"Are you sure there isn't time to change out of this wedding gown?"

"Positive." Xavier had to get her away before trouble really did come knocking, or before she started asking more pointed questions.

She snatched the veil from her head, grabbed her purse and started down the hall to the front door. "The door's still locked." A trace of fear returned to her voice. "How did you get in here?"

He inclined his head toward the sliding glass doors. "Balcony."

"We're three floors up!"

"I know." He reached past her and opened the door. "We'll take the stairs."

"But—" She bit back something that no doubt would have singed his ears and stepped into the quiet hallway. The fire door opened a second before they reached it.

Two men started to step into the hall and stopped dead to stare at him. He shoved Zoe behind him and yelled, "Run!"

DANI SINCLAIR

BODYGUARD TO THE BRIDE

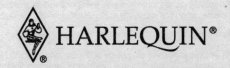

HARLEQUIN®

TORONTO • NEW YORK • LONDON
AMSTERDAM • PARIS • SYDNEY • HAMBURG
STOCKHOLM • ATHENS • TOKYO • MILAN • MADRID
PRAGUE • WARSAW • BUDAPEST • AUCKLAND

Some stories are easier to tell than others. This book would not have been possible without the help and support of my husband Roger, my good friends Judy Fitzwater and Robyn Pope, and my sister, Barbara. Thank you all!

ISBN-13: 978-0-373-69351-1
ISBN-10:   0-373-69351-6

BODYGUARD TO THE BRIDE

ABOUT THE AUTHOR

An avid reader, Dani Sinclair didn't discover romance novels until her mother lent her one when she'd come for a visit. Dani's been hooked on the genre ever since, but she didn't take up writing seriously until her two sons were grown. With the premiere of *Mystery Baby* for Harlequin Intrigue in 1996, Dani's kept her computer busy ever since. Her third novel, *Better Watch Out,* was a RITA® Award finalist in 1998. Dani lives outside Washington, D.C., a place she's found to be a great source for both intrigue and humor!

You can write to her in care of the Harlequin Reader Service.

Books by Dani Sinclair

HARLEQUIN INTRIGUE
730—THE FIRSTBORN**
736—THE SECOND SISTER**
742—THE THIRD TWIN**
827—SECRET CINDERELLA
854—D.B. HAYES, DETECTIVE
870—RETURN TO STONY RIDGE**
935—BEAUTIFUL BEAST
970—SLEEPING BEAUTY SUSPECT
1003—MIDNIGHT PRINCE
1084—BODYGUARD TO THE BRIDE

**Heartskeep

CAST OF CHARACTERS

Xavier Drake—This former Navy SEAL will do whatever it takes to save his niece.

Zoe Linden—Her groom is missing, her bodyguard is an enigma and someone wants her dead.

Wayne Drake—The affable charmer turned out to be a thief, but was he also a killer?

April Drake—The seven-year-old walked in on a robbery turned kidnapping.

Sandy Drake—Wayne's ex-wife doesn't trust the police to get her daughter back.

Eric Holmes—His job was to guard Zoe—until Xavier took his place.

Ike and Simon Schlosky—They have a vested interest in the briefcase Wayne stole.

Harrison Trent—The millionaire disappeared the night before his own wedding, and no one knows why, or where he is.

Artie Van Wheeler—He works with Zoe and Harrison, but how does he tie in to the kidnapping?

Chapter One

Xavier Drake stared at the woman in the full-length bedroom mirror. He hadn't expected her to be so lovely or so
delicate-looking. The cream-colored wedding gown with
its simple lines fell gracefully to the floor in soft folds. She
turned to the side, studying her reflection in profile. A
slender hand smoothed the satiny material against her
stomach. Brown hair, burnished to a gleaming teak, framed
her oval face.

He continued to watch in silence as she lifted the simple
veil from the top of her dresser and placed it on her head. All
the trite phrases people used to describe a bride flitted through
his mind. For the first time, he understood. Those phrases certainly described this bride-to-be. No wonder Wayne had been
so taken with this woman.

Her fawn-colored eyes widened in shock as their gazes met
in the mirror. Xavier was already moving forward as she
started to turn, lips parting.

"Don't scream," he ordered sternly. "I won't hurt you."

He got his hand over her mouth in time. She fought him
then, hampered by the dress. Even without that, she wouldn't
have had a chance. He was bigger, stronger, well trained in
unarmed combat and far more determined. His free arm

wrapped around her chest, pinning her right arm against a firm, full breast. Her left hand clawed his where it covered her mouth. She smelled faintly of cinnamon and vanilla.

"Don't make me drug you."

She stilled at the warning, chest heaving, eyes wide with fear in the mirror. He hated that he'd caused such a look, but he had little choice.

"I'm not going to rape you. I'm not going to hurt you at all if I can help it."

She breathed hard and fast through her nose. Her chest rose and fell beneath his arm. Her body was firm and strong, and she was a perfect height for him.

He shook off the thought. "I need you to come with me and we don't have much time. I'm going to let go of your mouth." He held her gaze sternly. "Don't scream. If you scream, I'll have to silence you. Do you understand?"

She gave a jerky nod.

"Do you promise not to scream?"

The nod came again, less jerky. Slowly, he released her mouth, ready to clamp down again if she drew a deep breath. Instead, the breath she drew was shaky. Eyes flashed in anger, still edged by fear.

"You nearly suffocated me! Let me go!"

"I don't think so."

"You said you weren't going to hurt me."

He relaxed his grip fractionally. "I'm not hurting you."

"My bruises say otherwise. How did you get in here?"

Someone must have told her a strong offense was the best defense. She was scared to death, but she had guts.

"Does it matter?"

Her eyes narrowed. "Harrison said you would stay outside."

"What?"

Still shaken, but now looking more annoyed than scared,

she shook her head. "Let me go. I'm sure Harrison didn't tell you to manhandle me."

He had no idea what she was talking about, but he was relieved and more than a little surprised that she was calm.

"I'll let you go as soon as I'm sure you aren't going to do anything stupid."

Her glare deepened. "Define *stupid*."

His lips twitched. "Screaming, running, trying to hit me with something."

"Deal."

He released her slowly. Immediately, she crossed to the nightstand. His hand closed over the telephone a moment before hers. "You agreed," he scolded.

"You didn't say anything about making a phone call. I want to talk to Harrison."

"Chew on him later. The others could show up any minute now."

"What others?"

"The men who killed Wayne know where you are. I saw one of them downstairs."

Her lips parted on a soft *oh* of comprehension. Her hand went to her stomach as fear widened her eyes once more. They were very pretty eyes.

"You saw one of them?"

"He was in the parking lot."

"It could have been someone who lives here."

"Or a thief looking for an unlocked car. You willing to take that chance?" Glancing around the room, he spotted a suitcase on the floor near the bed. "Is that case packed?"

"Mostly, yes. I still have a few more things in the dryer."

"Replace them later. Let's go."

"Like this? You're insane. I have to change!"

"Forget it. We don't have time. Consider this a formal kidnapping."

"But—"

"No *buts*. Lady, we have to go now. Every second you delay is costing precious time."

"The name is Zoe."

"I don't care if it's Fred." He grabbed the bag, wondering if it could possibly be this easy. Would she come with him willingly? "Let's go."

"At least let me change my shoes!"

There isn't time died unspoken. She was already stepping out of a pair of sexy slim high heels and sliding her feet into a pair of flat shoes on the floor nearby.

"I am not going to run around anywhere in those high heels. They pinch."

"Then why wear them?"

"They go with my gown. Are you sure there isn't time to change out of this dress?"

"Positive." He had to get her away before trouble really did come knocking or before she started asking more pointed questions—like how she could be sure he'd been sent by this Harrison person, who he assumed was probably the groom.

She snatched the wedding veil from her head, grabbed her purse from the foot of the bed and started down the hall to the living room. He followed, hefting a suitcase that weighed more than it should have given its size, amazed and relieved by this unexpected boon.

"The front door's still locked." A trace of fear returned to her voice as she flipped the dead bolt and looked back at him. "How *did* you get in here?"

He inclined his head toward the sliding glass doors. "The balcony."

"We're three floors up!"

"I know." He reached past her and opened the door. "Take the stairs. We'll go out the back."

"But—"

"Will you be quiet and move!"

She bit back something that no doubt would have singed his ears and stepped into the quiet hallway. Without further prompting, she headed for the stairwell. The fire door opened a second before they reached it. Two men started to step into the hall and stopped dead to stare at them. He shoved the woman behind him without glancing at her.

"Run!"

In slow motion, the larger one fumbled for a gun. Xavier slammed the suitcase into the wiry man in front. He staggered back, jostling the bigger one. The gun dropped from his hand. Xavier followed with a hard shove at the forward man's chest before either of them could go for the dropped weapon. Both men fell back onto the concrete landing.

Using the suitcase, Xavier slammed into the first man with all his strength and aimed a hard kick at his chest. The man fell back against his companion and both men tumbled down the concrete stairs. Spinning, Xavier opened the landing door that had closed at his back and ran down the hall toward Zoe.

The elevator came to a stop and the door slid open. With the skirt of her wedding gown bunched in her hand, Zoe held the door ajar, waiting. An older man started to step outside his apartment.

"Get back!" she yelled to him. "They have guns!"

The elderly man took in Xavier running down the hall with the suitcase, Zoe in her wedding dress and the gun on the carpeting behind him. Without a sound he darted back inside, slamming his door shut.

"Go!" Xavier ordered.

Footsteps pounded down the hall toward them. The elevator doors closed and Xavier pressed the button for Two.

"What are you doing?"

"Hoping they're dumb enough to run to the first floor."

"We'll be trapped!"

"Know anyone on Two?"

"Yes, but we can't put anyone else in danger."

He hit the button for One. "Think you can climb in that dress?"

"You have to be kidding. I'm getting married tomorrow. I can't get this dress dirty."

"If they kill you before morning, you won't have to worry about it, lady."

"I told you, the name is Zoe."

"Right." The door opened on Two. He stuck out his head. The sound of footsteps running down the concrete stairs was audible even from there. "Which apartment?"

"What?"

"Which apartment? You said you know people."

"227. Down the hall around the corner, but—"

"No *buts*, remember?"

Grabbing her hand, he tugged her in his wake. There was no sound from inside apartment 227 even after he rapped hard on the door.

"They probably aren't home," she told him breathlessly. "It's a Friday night."

"Good. Let's hope their dead bolt is as cheap as yours." Stepping back, he aimed a kick at the panel beside the doorknob.

"What are you doing?"

"Saving our lives." Three kicks and the door sprang open. Zoe gasped. Xavier hauled her inside and shut the broken door. "They'll need a new lock."

"Are you crazy?"

"Those men have guns," he reminded her.

"Don't you?"

"No." He scanned the dark interior, tugging her toward the balcony.

"What kind of bodyguard doesn't carry a gun?"

"The kind trying to save your life. Come on."

"What are you doing?"

"It isn't going to take them long to figure out where we went," he warned as he opened the balcony door. "Hopefully, right now that old man or one of your other neighbors is calling the police."

"I am not climbing off a second-story balcony," she panted.

He eyed her dress. "Yeah. Might be a stretch. I'll lower you."

Her hands went to her stomach. "No!"

Tossing her suitcase to the ground and grateful it didn't open and spill what had to be half the contents of her apartment, he grabbed her around the waist before she realized what he was going to do.

"No! Stop! I'll get hurt! I'll break something!"

"Make it your arm," he told her as he swung her, kicking and struggling over the railing. "You're going to need your legs to run."

"No!"

Xavier ignored her, lowering her as far down as he could. "Head for the parking lot. Don't stop and don't look back."

She shrieked as he let her go.

Zoe landed hard, momentarily stunned. Miraculously, she managed to stay on her feet. Her purse thumped heavily against her side as her veil fluttered to the ground. The bodyguard swung over the railing and leaped down as if it was something he did every day. Given the way he filled out his clothing, maybe it was.

Despite her earlier panic it had been impossible not to notice how lean, richly tanned and extremely fit he was. His hair was a wavy, golden brown with a tendency to curl. The hand he'd clamped over her mouth had been calloused and rough against her skin. It was a hand used to doing manual labor. And he was strong. Amazingly strong. He'd dangled her over that balcony as if she weighed nothing at all. She shuddered.

"Go!" he ordered. "You can have vapors later."

"I don't have vapors."

"Good. There isn't time."

Grabbing the suitcase in one hand, he yanked her hand and set off running. Zoe saved further protests. She needed her breath to keep up with him. And all she could think was it was good thing she'd had the sense to change shoes.

Part of her was wondering why she wasn't outright terrified. Shock, she decided. She'd seen the dropped gun and tonight wasn't the first attempt on her life. Vividly she recalled the sound of the shots being fired. She did her best to block out the sound of them striking flesh.

If the man leading her away had wanted her dead she wouldn't be running across the parking lot right now. Harrison had insisted on hiring a security firm to provide her with bodyguards, but she'd been so sure she'd be safe hiding here until the wedding. She hated that he'd been right to insist they stay on.

Funny how reassuring yet at the same time terrifying it was to know her bodyguard didn't carry a gun.

She owed Harrison her life twice over now. The only way to repay him was to be the best wife possible. She shoved down her misgivings as her bodyguard tossed her suitcase into the trunk of a small, dark coupe.

"Get in."

Zoe climbed carefully into the passenger's seat, trying to

keep her dress from wrinkling any further or touching anything that might get dirt on it.

She uttered a word her mother had always objected to.

"What?" he demanded, sliding in beside her.

"I left my shoes in the apartment. What am I going to wear in the morning?"

He muttered something under his breath and started the engine.

"Okay, I realize it isn't a life-and-death issue, but I can't get mar—"

He hadn't been muttering because she was lamenting her shoes. His gaze was on a third man running toward them, also holding a gun.

Her bodyguard peeled out of the parking space before she could fumble for the seat belt.

"How did they find me?"

"Good intel."

"What?" She gasped as he nearly sideswiped a minivan pulling into the parking lot. "Slow down! You nearly hit that— Ohmygod!"

He careened around a second vehicle and pulled onto the busy road without sparing oncoming traffic more than a glance. Zoe dropped the veil in her lap and braced her hands against the dashboard.

"You're insane! You're supposed to guard me, not kill me in a car wreck!"

"Relax."

"After the accident," she panted, "if we're still alive."

Teeth flashed as he grinned. The man had dimples! Bodyguards weren't supposed to have dimples. They should be ugly, hulking muscle men with squinty eyes. Although, come to think of it, who wanted squinty eyes? And there was nothing wrong with his muscles even if they weren't the bulging sort. In fact, there was nothing wrong with his looks at all. He had strong, rough-hewn features in a tanned face that needed a shave.

She closed her eyes and gripped her purse more tightly. She should not be noticing the way her bodyguard looked. Stress reaction, that's what it was. Too much stress. She was getting married in the morning.

The car swerved. She opened her eyes. Looking was better than not knowing if she was about to die. It was all she could do to keep quiet even though he handled the car with deft precision. They hadn't wrecked yet and he'd certainly had numerous opportunities.

And while she knew she shouldn't distract him, the light was changing up ahead and he wasn't slowing down!

Her hands clenched over her stomach. A gasp escaped despite her best efforts. Maybe not looking *was* better. Her stomach gave a warning twinge.

Not now. She could not be sick now.

Her stomach disagreed.

"Please." The word came out a prayer. Her dress would be ruined if she threw up all over it.

"Relax. We're clear. I'm slowing down."

Her stomach contracted. "Stop the car."

"What?"

"I'm going to be sick."

"It wasn't that close."

"Stop the car!" Zoe swallowed hard, tasting bile.

Closing her eyes, she gripped the veil in her lap so tightly she'd never get the wrinkles out. *Good. Think about that. Don't think about your stomach. Especially don't think about that greasy pizza you consumed for dinner.*

The car hit a bump. Her stomach gave an alarming lurch. Her eyes opened as the car pulled forward, backed up and rolled to a stop in a supermarket parking lot. Flinging open the door, she leaned as far out as possible, still wearing her seat belt, and allowed her stomach to have its way.

With a curse he was out of the car. She did not want to think about him standing on the tarred surface, watching her embarrass herself.

"Wait here," he ordered briskly.

Like she had a choice.

Trembling, Zoe fumbled in her purse for a bag of tissues, trying to ignore the nausea still plaguing the pit of her stomach. She couldn't have stuck with peanut butter on toast or a plain cheese pizza—oh, no. She had to go for the pepperoni and sausage swimming in grease.

She swallowed hard but it didn't help. There was nothing left to vomit, yet dry heaves racked her anyhow.

When she was finally able to bring the nausea under control, she blotted her mouth, leaned back and closed her eyes. Why couldn't she have been born with a cast-iron stomach like her friend Marge? Marge had eaten her way through three pregnancies without ever getting sick. But then again, Marge had never had anyone trying to kill her. And she'd never had to watch someone die just because they'd had the misfortune of standing beside her at the wrong moment.

Zoe sensed as much as heard someone approach the open car door. Her eyelids flew up.

"You okay?" The bodyguard was holding a brown plastic bag with the store's logo.

"Do I look okay?" Her mouth felt like the inside of a day-old sock, and her stomach still wasn't through with her.

"Here." He pulled a cold bottle of water from the bag and handed it to her.

"Thank you."

"Rinse out your mouth and spit."

"Charming." But she did exactly that. She felt marginally better with the bad taste gone and, bless him, he produced a travel-size bottle of mouthwash as well.

Humiliated, she glanced around. They were in an isolated spot well away from the nearest car. He'd backed the car in against a hedge of evergreens near the far side of the store. No one was paying them any attention.

Rinsing her mouth helped a great deal, but he wasn't finished. He produced a cloth, which he dampened with a second bottle of water and handed to her to wipe her face.

"I'm sorry," he apologized gruffly. "You might want to blot your dress. You have a spot."

Zoe couldn't look at him as she blotted the small splotch on her dress. Great. Perfect, even. She was going to get married in the morning in a dirty wedding dress and canvas shoes. Could this night get any better?

"I'm fairly certain we weren't followed. I should be able to take things slower now. Sit back and relax."

Zoe couldn't think of a thing to say. She took a small sip of water, savoring the cool trickle down her throat and did as instructed. Exhausted, she closed her eyes once more. He put a shopping bag on the backseat, closed her door and came around to slide behind the wheel once again.

Her mind coughed up all sorts of questions amid a swirl of thoughts, but she was too tired to ask anything right then. Her stomach was still grumpy and unsettled. Likely, she'd never eat another piece of pepperoni pizza as long as she lived. It was easiest to just sit there with her eyes closed and try not to think. There'd be time enough for answers when they reached Harrison.

She should have stayed at his penthouse from the start like he'd wanted her to do, but she'd wanted her own space and time to think after Wayne's death. Not that it had done her any good.

For a supposedly bright woman, she'd certainly played the idiot to perfection. First, letting herself be swept off her feet— literally—by handsome, fast-talking Wayne.

Somewhat like what had happened with her bodyguard tonight, now that she thought about it. *He* hadn't given her any time to think, either. But at least he hadn't tumbled her into bed with an ease that still amazed her.

Zoe cringed, remembering how rash she'd been. She hadn't wanted to go to Harrison's party in the first place. Once a month, she met with her friends Sharon, Marge and Helen for a girl's night out. They usually went for dinner and a movie or to a play. Going to a party hadn't been part of their plans, but Harrison had insisted she come and bring them as well, and the others had liked the idea.

The party had been crowded, the music loud, the beer cold and the dancing fun. Zoe could still remember the way Wayne had looked when he'd asked her to dance. Tall and sexy, his dirty-blond hair styled just so, eyes gleaming and a smile that hit a woman right where she lived.

Her friends, happily imbibing the freely flowing liquor, had egged her on and they'd soon had their own partners. Wayne had danced every dance with her after the first few, and they'd talked and laughed away the entire evening. Her friends had been nearly forgotten beneath Wayne's steady charm. Zoe had given him her phone number, but she hadn't let him take her home.

Not that night.

He'd called while she was getting ready for bed and they'd talked until she had started to doze off from sheer weariness. She'd never known anyone like him. He'd said all the right things, flattering her outrageously, soon buying her silly gifts she couldn't turn down—like the mug with all the funny sayings. If he'd sent her roses instead of daisies she'd have been leery, but he'd known to bring her M&M's instead of expensive chocolates.

He'd pursued her with a single-minded determination that had been fun and exciting as well as flattering. And look where it had gotten her. Her hand went to her stomach. She opened her eyes as the car glided to a stop.

Fear gripped her hard as she looked around at yet another dark parking lot.

"Where are we?"

"My motel. And before you panic, I promise I have no designs on you. I thought you might want to change out of that dress before you go anywhere else."

He held out a key card. "I need to make a phone call. Then we need to talk. All right?"

"No. I want to see Harrison."

"Looking like that?"

"What's wrong with how I look?" She glanced down at her dress. The veil rested on the floor at her feet where she'd dropped it to lean outside the car.

"If I say not a thing, will you take it the wrong way?"

His voice was even, his expression unreadable, but she felt a funny tingle nonetheless.

"I'll wait outside in the hall. I have no intention of jumping you."

"I didn't think you did."

And that was only partly a lie. Once more, Zoe told herself that if he'd wanted to hurt her, he'd had his chance earlier. Still…

"Why did you bring me here?"

"It was on the way."

"Oh."

Was she being an idiot once again, trusting this stranger? There was nothing threatening in his manner. At least, not now, but she couldn't forget how he'd grabbed her, threatened her with drugs, kicked down a door and sped through city streets like a racer gone mad. Going into a motel with a man as dangerous as this one seemed like a really stupid thing to do. On the other hand, she did want out of this dress and she was strangely unafraid of this man.

"It's your call, la…Zoe."

"You'll wait in the hall?"

"I said I would."

"Okay." She could always scream. The parking lot around them was close to full and busy with people coming and going. And the first thing she was going to do once she got inside was put the dead bolt on and call Harrison.

He carried her suitcase across the lot to a side door. She followed him inside and up the concrete stairs to the second floor, ignoring the looks she was certain they were drawing. Exhaustion was making her muzzy. The past four months of stress had taken their toll. She was so tired she could sleep for a week.

XAVIER SET THE SUITCASE inside on the king-size bed and fished out his cell phone while she stood at the open door. "I'll be outside. Call me when you're ready."

Stepping past her into the hall, he leaned back against the wall and heard the dead bolt click into place. He strode briskly down the stairs to the main floor. At the desk he asked for a second key card to his room. The harried clerks seemed almost relieved by the simple request. The telephone kept ringing and a boisterous group of people approached as Xavier showed his identification.

Key card in hand, Xavier started back up the stairs. He hit Speed Dial and waited for Sandy to pick up.

"I got her," he told his former sister-in-law without preamble.

"Thank God." Excitement filled her husky voice. "You didn't have any trouble?"

"Nothing I couldn't handle. You were right though. Wayne's partners *did* show up."

She sucked in a breath. "Partners, plural? Did they say anything to you? What happened?"

"We didn't have time for a conversation. I shoved the two who came inside down a flight of stairs, grabbed the woman and left."

"Where are you?"

"At my motel."

"You were supposed to take her to Wayne's place."

"Change of plan. She thinks I'm a bodyguard sent by Harrison. I take it he's the groom?"

"Yes," she agreed absently. "What's wrong with going to Wayne's apartment? You could tell her Harrison Trent wanted you to take her there for safekeeping."

"There were three men altogether, Sandy."

"Three?"

"Maybe more. I saw three. If there are more they could have someone watching your place and Wayne's apartment for all we know. Let's not take chances. When they call, tell them we have her and arrange a meet."

Her voice rose another octave. "What if something goes wrong?"

"I'll handle it."

He sensed she wanted to argue, but for once she settled for a ragged sigh. "I don't know what I'd do if you hadn't shown up today, Xavier."

"It's going to be fine, Sandy." It had to be fine. He couldn't stand thinking about what might be happening to his niece. "Arrange the meet and let me deal with them."

"But what if…? All right. I'm just scared. She's so young."

He heard her the ragged edge of fear in her voice and his fingers tightened on the cell phone. "April's a bright kid. They won't hurt her." His body tensed. He prayed it was true. "She'll be fine."

"You're right. I know you are. I'll call you as soon as I hear from them."

"You won't do her any good if you make yourself sick. Try to rest."

"I'll try."

He disconnected as he reached the second floor. By now the bride would have called Harrison. She'd know Xavier hadn't been sent by him. He was literally betting his life that neither she nor Harrison would call the police.

Xavier shook his head. The woman *would* try to get away, however, and he had to keep that from happening. There was too much at risk, including the life of a seven-year-old little girl.

Chapter Two

Xavier started to insert the card in the door when the lock clicked inside and it flew open in his face. He leaned back, prepared for anything.

"I can't reach Harrison!"

Okay, *that* he hadn't been prepared for. He'd expected fury, recriminations, fear, but that she wouldn't be able to reach her fiancé wasn't something he'd considered.

"Inside," he ordered.

She backed up at his firm tone and allowed him to enter the room. Xavier knew most people were conditioned to respond automatically to authority and he used it without a qualm.

Zoe still wore her wedding gown. The dress hugged her upper curves like a lover and the satin flowed over her hips. It was a very sexy gown on her. The veil lay on the bed beside a pair of dark slacks and a peach blouse.

"At least you thought about changing clothes."

"What?"

And she didn't look so deathly pale anymore. He ignored another twinge of regret and steeled his heart. Her soft brown hair was tousled as if she'd been running fingers through the thick strands.

"Don't you understand? Harrison isn't answering his cell

phone. He *always* answers his cell phone. It's practically implanted in his ear."

"Maybe he's busy."

"It's turned off! The call goes straight to voice mail."

"There you go. He's busy *and* he turned it off."

She had perfected the art of glaring. "He *never* turns it off. Something's wrong."

Xavier tipped his head. "Not necessarily."

"What if they went after him to get to *me!*"

He shook his head. "They already knew where you were, remember?"

Zoe began to pace in front of the double beds. "Maybe that's how they learned where I was."

"You think he'd tell them?"

She stopped pacing. Shoving at the strands of hair, she tucked some behind her ear and shook her head. "No. You're right. Harrison wouldn't tell them anything. Chivalry is his middle name."

Xavier frowned. The words were right but her tone seemed off, considering she was talking about the man she was about to marry.

"I'm surprised he didn't come himself," she continued, "especially if he knew they found out where I was. Why didn't he call to warn me?" She resumed pacing.

Zoe did not sound like a woman in love.

"We need to go see him." She stopped pacing and turned to face him.

"We can't do that."

"You're my bodyguard, not my jailer."

"I take my job seriously."

"Even if it means dropping me off a balcony?"

"Even then," he agreed, matching her irony.

"You threatened to drug me."

He shrugged. "Expediency. I don't have any drugs."

"Is that what they teach you in bodyguard school? Use any means available?" Her voice rose along with her anger. "Bullying, threats, even dropping your subjects off balconies?"

He flashed a grin, hoping to diffuse her before she built up a full head of mad. "You're really hung up on that balcony, aren't you?"

"I could have been hurt!"

"You could have been dead," he reminded her.

"Well, I'm not spending the night in a motel room with a man I don't know."

Showtime. He'd been winging things from the moment he'd laid eyes on her. His original intention to shake answers out of her had fled the moment he'd seen a man get out of a car in the parking lot and check his gun. Xavier realized then that she was potentially in danger, too. Now he wasn't sure what approach to take with her.

His sister-in-law believed Zoe was a thief like his late brother, Wayne. Sandy had even suggested Zoe had had Wayne murdered to gain what he'd stolen. Having met Zoe, Xavier had a hard time believing that. But what if he was wrong?

His jaw tightened. "The name's Xavier. Xavier Drake."

It took her a moment. Color leached from her face as his last name finally registered. "Drake? As in Wayne Drake?"

"My brother."

She sank down on the end of the bed like a deflated balloon. "I didn't know he had a brother."

"Brother, sisters, parents, aunts, uncles, nieces, nephews, even a daughter," he bit out.

Her head jerked up. "Wayne had a daughter?"

"And an ex-wife."

Her lips parted. She started to say something and stopped.

Her eyes closed. Hands went to her stomach. She looked ill. "I didn't know."

Xavier believed her. No one was that good an actress.

"He had a daughter and he never mentioned her."

She said it to herself rather than to him. Her pained expression revealed hurt, betrayal and recrimination. But not anger. Surely there would have been anger or satisfaction if she had ordered his brother killed as Sandy believed.

Xavier knew his brother. Wayne had had enough charisma for twenty politicians. He'd also shared some of their more flexible views of right and wrong. Looking at Zoe's stricken features, Xavier automatically softened his voice. "April's seven years old."

ZOE'S MIND SPUN WITH shock. Nausea made her want to curl into a ball and pull the covers over her head.

"Did she live with him?"

"No. April lives with her mother."

The hint of sympathy in his stern features only made Zoe feel worse. "How long have they been divorced?"

"I'm not sure when it became final. Probably a few weeks ago."

"Weeks?" She had met Wayne over four months ago. He'd told her he wasn't married and she'd believed him. How could she have been so stupid? Every single thing Wayne had told her had been a lie. She stared at his brother. Abruptly, the truth hit her. "Harrison didn't send you to protect me, did he?"

"No."

Cold fear settled over her. "Where's the man he did send and why—"

"I need the briefcase Wayne gave you."

She frowned, puzzled. "What briefcase? He never gave me a briefcase." Her mind raced as she stared at his implacable features. Were the two really related? She couldn't see any resemblance, except that this man was probably every bit the liar his brother was. "You're a thief, too?"

Anger tightened his sun-bronzed features. For the second time that night she felt afraid of him.

"Stealing was my brother's occupation, not mine."

There was truth in every rigid, affronted line of his lean body.

"You knew he was a thief?" he added harshly.

Wearily, she shook her head at the accusation. "Not until the police told me. After…after he was killed, they wanted to know what he'd been doing." She shook her head. "I didn't know. He'd told me he was an investment counselor."

"Investing in other people's belongings," Xavier agreed, his voice hard and bitter.

"Did he steal from you, too?"

"Let's just say my brother believed in finders keepers no matter how far out of his way he went to 'find' things."

Flat, hard, uncompromising. From his tone, Xavier obviously felt only contempt for his dead brother. Zoe no longer knew what she felt for Wayne. Their brief time together had taken on a dreamlike, almost surreal feeling.

"You don't look like him."

She hadn't meant to say that out loud even though it was true. Wayne had been incredibly handsome. Not that Xavier wasn't good-looking, but Wayne had been leading-man handsome, not ruggedly confident handsome like this man. Wayne had oozed charm and polish. He had always been meticulously well dressed. Zoe couldn't picture Wayne dressed in a tired pair of jeans and an open-necked shirt. Not even if they'd had designer labels.

Xavier's didn't. He wore relaxed, lived-in clothing that suited him far more than the perfectly fitted suits and expensive ties his brother had favored. Xavier in a tie was a stretch for her imagination.

"Wayne took after our mother," Xavier told her. "I look like our dad."

Xavier Drake was at home in his own skin. Obviously comparisons only bothered him when someone took him for a thief as well.

"My brother liked to shower his women with gifts."

Zoe cringed at *his women,* but hadn't she always secretly wondered why Wayne had singled her out when he could have had anyone at all? She was comfortable with her looks and knew how to make the most of them. Still, at the party where they'd met there had been other women present who had been as stunning in their way as Wayne had been in his. Her friend Helen, for example, had modeled professionally for a living. Yet Wayne had culled Zoe from the pack and flattered her outrageously while her friends had drooled with envy.

"Wayne knew not to give me expensive gifts," she told him. "He gave me things like M&M's and daisies and a funny mug, a tiny music box, a stuffed monkey, that sort of thing."

She hadn't needed expensive gifts to fall into bed with him after only two dates, and she never did things like that. She hadn't been able to justify her actions to herself even when it had been happening. There was no way she could explain that to this strong, silent man so unlike his charismatic brother.

Xavier shook his head. "He must have given you something."

"Nothing of value. Oh! Except the ring."

He came to attention, cocking his head and waiting.

"He…your brother asked me to marry him." She shifted uncomfortably at the memory. She hadn't wanted to meet Wayne that night. By then she'd been publicly engaged to Harrison, but he'd pleaded. Just dinner in a public place. And she'd known she had to see him one last time despite Harrison's warning.

She'd been totally unprepared for a proposal. The words had come out of the blue and had sent a wave of cold right through her. Wayne had always moved too fast, and she'd already learned he didn't like no for an answer.

"We were in the restaurant that night...before it happened." She would not think about the sound of the shots or the way he'd lain bleeding in her arms, looking so surprised. "I wasn't expecting it."

Not any of it. Not the proposal, not the gunshots outside the restaurant, not the sudden impossible death of the man who'd just asked her to be his wife despite the ring already gleaming on her finger.

"He told me he loved me." She shuddered as memory washed over her.

"So you were dating him while you were engaged to Trent?"

"No!" Heat claimed her cheeks at the trace of scorn in his voice. She knew what he was thinking. How could she blame him? She *had* gone from one man to another, but it wasn't the way he was thinking.

"Are you saying you turned my brother down?" This time his voice conveyed disbelief.

Zoe lifted her chin defiantly. She refused to feel guilty or ashamed. "What happened between me and your brother is none of your business."

He stared without saying a word. She didn't need to explain a thing to him, but she found herself doing so anyway.

"I met your brother four months ago. We dated for a couple of weeks, and I broke it off." And she did not want to relive that scene even in her thoughts.

"*You* broke it off?"

Her jaw set at his mocking tone. Zoe used the glare she had

perfected for dealing with difficult clients who felt women had no place in the business world. "Yes, I broke it off. Your brother moved way too fast for me."

Xavier rocked back on his heels. He studied her as if trying to read the truth in her words. "Wayne always did go full bore after what he wanted."

She hated the sudden need to defend Wayne and herself. "Your brother was funny and—"

"Charming. Yeah. I know."

Charming was an understatement. Wayne had made Zoe feel like the most special, cherished person in the world. He'd showered her with incredibly flattering attention. But that charm had been overpowering. And flawed.

Still, even after the police had told her he had a criminal record, Zoe had had trouble reconciling that knowledge with the man she'd known. Part of her still did, despite watching him die in her arms and seeing his rap sheet on the police computer.

"How did you hook up with him in the first place?" Xavier asked.

She bristled defensively, then took a calming breath. He hadn't said *someone like you* although the words had been implied by his tone.

"I met your brother at a party. Wayne told me he'd come with a friend. It wasn't until after he died that I learned he'd lied. The police believe he crashed the party to steal something or case the penthouse for a future robbery." She didn't want to continue, but Xavier had already lumped her with Wayne's other conquests.

"The man I work for… It was Harrison's party. He's wealthy and so are most of his friends. I'm his assistant."

"And now his fiancée."

He didn't sneer, but her skin heated all the same. The change in status was already an uncomfortable adjustment for her. She shook her head, aware of how this probably sounded to the man in front of her.

"Frankly, I think Wayne wanted me only because it would have given him access to a number of wealthy people. Even the police believe that's why he latched on to me in the first place." Her cheeks continued to blaze. It was difficult to admit to this self-assured man what a complete idiot she'd been.

"So you weren't engaged to Trent when you were dating my brother?"

"Of course not!" Angrily, Zoe stood. Her body trembled, and that would never do. Her hand went to her stomach. She took a deep breath and reminded herself that she didn't care what this man thought of her. "I don't owe you any explanations."

"No, you don't," he agreed easily. "You can marry whom-ever you want, lady. All I want is the briefcase or whatever was inside."

"I told you, Wayne didn't give me a briefcase. He didn't give me anything of value except the diamond ring. And you're welcome to that. I don't want it. I never did."

"The ring was probably stolen."

Her heart constricted. She hadn't considered that. But then she hadn't been thinking straight since the night she'd met Wayne Drake. It was time to stop reacting and become pro-active. "How do I even know you're Wayne's brother?"

He slid a hand into his hip pocket and produced a worn leather wallet. Flipping it open, he held it out. Zoe took it, careful not to touch him. The photo on the driver's license wasn't flattering, but it was definitely him.

"This is a Florida driver's license."

He tilted his head in acknowledgment. "That's where I live. My family runs a charter boat service out of a little town north of Boca Raton. We specialize in fishing and pleasure cruises. It's a family business but Wayne wasn't interested."

"He didn't like boats," she agreed, handing the wallet back. His hand brushed hers this time and her skin tingled at the contact. "He mentioned that once."

"Look, lady…Zoe…Wayne had partners. They want whatever he stole on his last job."

Her heart thundered in her chest. "The police never said—"

"Hopefully, the police don't have any idea what he'd been up to lately and I'd just as soon keep it that way for now." He ran a hand over his jaw.

"I don't understand." She was so tired. It was hard to think at all.

"It's simple. I need to find what Wayne stole before his partners do."

"Why? If you aren't a thief…"

He measured her with dark, dangerous eyes. Her heart skipped a beat at the angry impatience she sensed simmering below the surface. His voice hardened when he spoke, and the hairs rose along her arms.

"His partners took my niece. I'm going to get her back. You're going to help me."

The stark words took a moment to sink in. "Are you saying she was kidnapped?"

"Yes."

Horror gripped her. "Why?"

"They want to trade her life for what they think you have."

For a second she couldn't breathe. "That's insane."

"They're criminals." He shrugged. "They don't have to make sense. They think Wayne gave you whatever they stole."

"But he didn't!"

"You're sure?"

The icy menace in his tone sent a shiver straight down her spine. She forced herself to hold his dark, piercing gaze. "I'm positive."

For a long moment he didn't move. Neither did she. She refused to look away, willing him to believe her.

"Too bad they don't know that."

Zoe put her face in her hands. Her stomach was clenched so tight that the sick feeling nearly overwhelmed her again.

"We'll have to risk going back to your place and hope they aren't still watching."

She lifted her head at his words. "The only briefcase I have belongs to me. And it isn't at the apartment."

"Where is it?"

"At Harrison's. I was only staying in that condo until after the wedding. It isn't mine and I don't have many belongings there. Harrison moved most of my things to his place after the burglary."

"What burglary?"

Things began tumbling into place. "My condo was burglarized shortly after Wayne…died. His partners must be the ones who broke in."

His scowl was fierce. "When was this?"

"A few nights after Wayne died. We aren't exactly sure. I didn't stay there after his murder."

His expletive made her flinch. "They didn't get what they're looking for so they think you still have it."

"But I don't! I never had Wayne's briefcase, or anything that belonged to him."

"Are you telling me he never spent the night with you?"

His incredulous tone made her furious. Who was he to judge her?

"Wayne never did like to sleep alone," he stated calmly. "He must have taken his case to your place once or twice."

Had he? She couldn't remember.

"Did your fiancé move everything Wayne gave you to his place?" he continued.

"Yes, but I told you, they were small items, not valuables."

"These people aren't going to all this work for a cheap coffee mug. Wayne had something of value and they want it. The two of you were an item so you're the obvious person to have it if it wasn't at his place. Looks like you get your wish, lady. Let's go see your fiancé."

"I need to throw up again."

"ARE YOU COMING DOWN with something?" Xavier asked when Zoe finally opened the bathroom door. She looked as wan and as pale as death but she offered him one of those glares that probably went over well in the boardroom. "Here, drink some of this."

She accepted the cola he'd gone to get from the machine down the hall and took a tentative sip. After a moment she began to drink.

"Hey, go easy on that. My mother claims cola soothes upset stomachs but I don't think you're supposed to chug it."

She really did look exhausted. Xavier was oddly tempted to comfort her. Only the thought of what his niece might be going through stopped him. Easy to see why his brother and this Harrison Trent guy were drawn to her. Zoe Linden wasn't beautiful, but she was pretty in a way that brought out his protective instincts even when it was obvious she wasn't as fragile as she seemed.

"Thank you," she told him.

He regarded her uncomfortably. "Look, I hate to push you when you're sick—"

Her chin came up. "I'm not sick. I'm pregnant. Let's go."

Xavier's gaze flew to her stomach. Maybe it was a little rounded, but he never would have guessed she was pregnant. "You don't look pregnant."

"Thank you, Dr. Drake. Shall we go if we're going?"

He recovered enough to look pointedly at her gown. "Don't you think you should change first? I believe it's still considered bad luck for the groom to see the bride in her wedding dress before the wedding."

She glanced down as if surprised by the dress she wore. "Oh."

Snatching up the clothes on the end of the bed, she retreated back into the bathroom.

"I'll just be a minute."

Amazingly, she was true to her words. The loose blouse and slacks looked as good on her as the fancy wedding dress had. And she still didn't look pregnant. He'd have said elegantly casual, if there was such a thing. But no wonder she'd been so upset when he'd dropped her off the balcony.

"You should have told me you were pregnant," he complained as he opened the door to their room. "I dropped you off a balcony."

"I remember."

"I could have hurt you."

She started for the stairs they'd used coming in. "I believe I mentioned that at the time."

"But I didn't know you were pregnant."

She stopped walking. "Did we have another choice?"

"I'd have found one."

"Then next time I'll mention it."

She started walking again. He swallowed a retort, trying to remember if his sisters had been this moody when they'd been pregnant. She didn't say another word as they went down the steps, but he stopped her before she reached the outside door. "Let me go first."

"Why not? You make a much larger target."

His lips nearly curved. She had spunk.

Xavier stepped into the warm summer night and scanned the dimly lit parking lot. A couple with a fussy child had just pulled up. Two couples in a van parked across the way, killing their loud radio. They made up for it with noisy conversation as they climbed out. A man and a woman came around the building together, heading for a parked sports car. A dark sedan pulled up out front. Nothing alarming in any of it. As far as Xavier could see, no one was sitting in a car or lurking in the shadows watching the building.

He motioned to Zoe and she joined him on the sidewalk. Together they crossed the open lot to where he'd parked.

An engine revved. He looked up to see the dark-colored sedan speeding down the parking lot without headlights. It was headed straight at them.

Xavier shoved Zoe down alongside his car. Weapons fire was loud in his ears as he landed on top of her.

Chapter Three

Someone in the parking lot began to scream. The car sped past, tires squealing as it turned the corner of the building, racing up the other side.

"Get off me!"

Xavier was already springing to his feet. The car was a blur disappearing onto the main road.

"Is the baby okay?"

"I'm fine. Thank you for asking."

A man ran toward them. Xavier hauled Zoe to her feet, flung open the passenger door and shoved her inside. "Keep down!"

"Anyone hurt?" the man asked.

"Just shaken up." He moved forward to meet the man before he could get too close to Zoe. "How about you?"

"We're fine. My wife's calling the cops. You sure you and your wife are all right?"

"We were on our way to the hospital anyhow. She ate some bad chicken for dinner. You should get everyone inside until the police arrive. That nutcase may come back around."

The man nodded. He ran back to the woman waiting nervously by the door, speaking into a cell phone.

Xavier ran to the driver's side and slid in.

"Why did you tell him I was sick?" Zoe demanded.

"I didn't want him thinking we were the targets. He might have made a note of our license plate. If he thinks this was a random shooting he won't bother. *Are* you okay?"

"A scrape." She sat up straighter.

"I told you to stay down."

"Why? He's gone." But she did as he'd ordered, slouching on the seat.

"Like I told that guy, he could come back."

Xavier drove off as quickly as he dared, passing the man and his wife. They were talking to several other people inside the building's doorway. The minute he pulled onto the main road he accelerated.

"Did you see who was driving?" she asked.

"I was busy shoving you out of the way."

"I know. Thank you, but you could have just told me to duck."

Despite her brave words he saw that she was trembling.

"Did you at least get the make of the car?"

He shook his head. "It was small, black or dark blue."

"I thought guys knew all about cars."

"I know boats, okay? It wasn't a boat."

"No, a boat would have stood out."

"You've got a weird sense of humor, lady."

"Zoe. And so I've been told. You're bleeding!"

He followed her wide-eyed stare as they passed under a streetlight. Blood ran down his arm from his tricep. He swore softly, only now feeling the burning sting.

"You've been shot!"

"I might have injured my arm on the car mirror."

"Stop the car so I can have a look."

"I want to get well away from here first. It's just a scratch."

"Scratches don't bleed like that."

Or generally hurt like the devil, he could have added. She fished in her purse and pulled out a package of tissues.

"I'll look at it while you drive."

"I don't think those things are going to do much good."

She burrowed back inside her purse. "I have a hand sanitizer with alcohol. At least I can clean it out so you don't get an infection. Oh! And I have a handkerchief."

"Blood will ruin it."

"You can buy me a new one."

He hadn't anticipated anyone shooting at them. But he probably should have. He knew the men had guns. Only, why would they risk killing her when they wanted information from her?

Because they weren't shooting at *her*. He was the one they'd shot. Take him out and she became more vulnerable.

Distracted by her hands on his arm, he studied the headlights behind them. There was too much traffic to tell if they were being followed.

"I need directions to your fiancé's place."

"Your arm needs to be bandaged. I think this is what they call a graze in the movies. I don't think it's serious but it's hard to tell with all this blood."

"Sorry, rental cars don't come with first-aid kits."

"Well, they should. And if you pass out from blood loss you aren't going to do me much good."

His lips curved. "It isn't that bad."

"Right. Turn left at the next traffic light."

His arm hurt in earnest as she pressed on the wound. It was still bleeding when they reached the underground lot of a tall condominium in the high-rent district. Zoe produced a card that got them inside the garage and directed him to a prime, well-lit spot near an elevator that resembled a pair of intricately carved wooden doors. Discreetly placed cameras watched every move as they climbed out of his car.

"Harrison's Ferrari is gone."

Xavier eyed the silver Mercedes parked next to the empty space she'd indicated. His little rental car looked like an ugly duckling beside the expensive luxury cars surrounding it.

Zoe inserted the card in a slot beside the elevator. The doors swished silently open, revealing a surprisingly large interior.

"What do *you* drive?" he asked her.

"A BMW, why?"

"Curiosity. Aren't we missing a few buttons to press?"

"This elevator only goes to the penthouse."

Of course it did. And the intricate trim on the inside of the elevator was no doubt real gold leaf.

She lifted the telephone. "Try not to drip blood on the carpet."

He eyed the thick dark carpet underfoot and raised his eyebrows. "Right. I'll give it my best."

In the mirrored back panel he saw that the injury was a shallow crease with a chunk of missing skin. Not the car's mirror, then. The crease continued to well with thick, red blood. She hung up, looking worried.

"What's wrong?"

"Leon isn't answering."

"And Leon would be?"

"Harrison's housekeeper."

A housekeeper named Leon. "Doesn't that make him a butler? Or is Leon a woman?"

"He's six foot four and used to play pro football."

"Right. Probably not a woman. If he isn't answering, does that mean we can't get inside?"

"No." Worry lined her face. "But Leon should be answering."

"Maybe he has the night off."

"His car was downstairs."

"The silver Mercedes?"

"No, the Mercedes is Harrison's. Leon owns the green Porsche."

"Your fiancé's housekeeper played pro ball and drives a green Porsche?"

"Yes."

Xavier couldn't wait to meet Harrison Trent. The doors opened on a vast marble foyer with elaborate chandeliers that weren't lit and fancy dim wall sconces that were. Still frowning, Zoe used her key card again to let them through a wide set of double doors. A vast, open room with high ceilings and a wall of windows looked over the twinkling lights of Arlington and beyond that, D.C. across the Potomac spread before them. Two small lamps glowed softly. Without them the room would have been in total darkness.

"Leon? Harrison?"

Zoe flicked on more lights as she called out. The room was decorated in elegant soft creams and rich wood tones that had a masculine flavor with feminine touches, such as the vases of fresh cut flowers.

"Nice place."

"Leon!"

The furniture looked comfortably enticing given the fatigue that was starting to set in. "Doesn't look like anyone's home. Bathroom?"

"This way."

Xavier pressed the handkerchief more tightly against his wound, hoping he wouldn't track blood on the highly polished teak floors or the rich, thick rugs.

The powder room was equally intimidating. A handblown glass bowl replaced the usual basin, and water sprouted from a fancy gold designer spigot. He met his tired gaze in the wood-framed oval mirror and decided he could use a shave, a haircut and twelve hours of uninterrupted sleep.

"No offense, but I don't think your Harrison would want me to use his monogrammed towels for this. That's probably real gold thread. Leon would never get the bloodstains out."

"Harrison can afford new towels."

She reached for one and wrapped it around his bloody arm. "Hold this there with some pressure. I'll be right back."

Xavier decided his bloodstained T-shirt was a write-off so he pulled it over his head and examined the cut. It still oozed, but no longer welled with blood. Since Zoe had already ruined the towel, he wet it down and held it against the graze, applying pressure.

By the time Zoe returned with a first-aid kit a few minutes later, the bleeding had slowed. Her expressive eyes took in his tanned, bared chest with a flush of feminine appreciation. Working on boats as he did, Xavier was used to women appraising him with his shirt off, but her gaze felt more intimate in this setting.

She lowered her lashes and set about briskly opening packages of gauze, tape, alcohol rubs and ointment.

"You're enjoying this."

Her gaze flashed to his face. The flush deepened. Steel entered her expression and her tone. "Of course I am. There's nothing I want to do more on the eve of my wedding."

And there was nothing he could say to that.

"That shirt's a total loss."

"That's what I figured," he agreed. "Think your Harrison would mind if I borrowed one of his? I promise to clean it and get it back to him."

"I'll find something. Hold still. This is going to sting."

It did, but she was quick and efficient as she washed the cut, wiped it with an alcohol rub and coated it with ointment before covering it with a gauze pad and binding it tightly.

While she worked, Xavier decided the vanilla scent came from her hair. The cinnamon scent must be on her skin.

"What are you doing?"

"What?"

"Were you sniffing me?"

He shrugged. "You smell nice."

She took a step back, ducked her head and busied her hands packing away the first-aid supplies. "Thank you."

"You're welcome."

"I tried calling Harrison's cell phone again. He still isn't answering."

"Any sign of a disturbance in here?"

"Not down here, but I didn't go upstairs."

"There's an upstairs? I thought this was the penthouse."

"It is. There's a partial second floor. That's where the bedrooms and greenhouse are."

"A greenhouse."

She looked uncomfortable. "Leon likes to garden."

"Of course he does. I bet he cooks, too."

"At least one five-star restaurant has tried to hire him. Come on. We need to get you a shirt."

Xavier rinsed out the stained towel and used his shirt to wipe the sink before placing it in the fancy trash can and following her to an open staircase. Two enormous bedroom suites and a large sitting room overlooked a sizable greenhouse, large deck, pool and outdoor bar.

"Okay, I'm impressed."

"Yes, it's a bit much."

Once again she didn't sound like a woman in love. Was pregnancy making her irritable or were they getting married only because of the baby?

"Harrison had Leon put my things in here. I'll go get you a shirt."

Most of Xavier's small house could have fit inside this single bedroom with space to spare. There was no personal stamp on the room or its furnishings and the huge walk-in closet held only women's clothing. He had to wonder if Harrison was only storing her belongings in here until after the wedding or if the two of them were planning on separate bedrooms.

A number of neatly marked boxes sat along the window wall with its different view of the city.

"Here. This should fit."

He took the maroon, short-sleeved polo shirt she held out and raised his eyebrows at the insignia over the left breast.

"No T-shirts?"

"Hey, you want to be picky, go raid his closet yourself. I grabbed the first casual shirt I saw."

"Right." He slipped it on while she began opening boxes, quickly rooting through the contents. The items she pulled out were exactly as stated—a mug, a stuffed monkey, a novelty picture frame sans picture. Simple, inexpensive items. The briefcase she dug out of another box was good-quality leather with discreet initials monogrammed in one corner, *ZEL*.

"What's the *E* stand for?"

"Elizabeth, why?"

He shrugged. "Just curious."

The briefcase was filled with the sort of papers and accoutrements a busy working woman might carry. He closed it and set it on the dresser.

"This is everything he gave you?"

"Except the flowers and the M&M's. Oh! And the ring!"

She did some more searching, found another box and a box inside the box.

"Is this like those Russian stacking dolls?" he asked as she pulled out yet another box before getting to a small ring box. That one she proffered to him. Xavier blinked as he opened it and gazed down at the ostentatious ring. "Nice."

He didn't know much about diamonds, but Xavier didn't need to be an expert to see that this was an expensive stone and setting.

"Do you really think it's stolen?"

"Most likely." He closed the box, his anxiety building. "Wayne liked to do his shopping in other people's homes. And as pricey as I'm sure this is, I don't see this ring being what his partners are after." It had been a long shot, after all. He started to hand it back but Zoe shook her head.

"Keep it. I don't want it."

"Wouldn't fit me." He set the box on the end of the bed. "Could Wayne have hidden something in your place without you knowing—maybe inside a mattress or a chair or something?"

"The people who tore my condo apart thought of that. They sliced open every stick of furniture I had. We had to send almost everything to the dump. What was left we gave to the Salvation Army. There wasn't much."

Xavier muttered under his breath.

"Go ahead and look through whatever you want. Everything from my condo is in these boxes. I'll be right back."

Surveying the room, Xavier tried to put himself in his brother's position. If Wayne had wanted to hide something of real value, what would he have done? Xavier would have taken out a safety-deposit box, but if his brother had had a safety-deposit box it would have come to light by now.

Xavier picked up the stuffed animal and squeezed it, probing for loose threads or the feel of something inside. Nothing. He'd hoped Wayne's partners had missed something when they'd destroyed Zoe's place, but it seemed unlikely. At least they had known what they were searching for. He didn't have a clue.

His cell phone rang and Sandy's cell-phone number appeared. "Sandy?"

"Xavier, where are you? Have you found the briefcase?"

He wished he had something positive to offer her. "No. I'm sorry, Sandy. We're still looking."

"*We?* I can't believe you think *she's* going to help you."

"Sandy—"

"Xavier, she *has* to be involved! His partners wouldn't have killed Wayne before they got their cut unless they trusted her to give them their share. It's the only thing that makes sense. She was standing right beside him when he was murdered, yet she walked away without a scratch. It had to be a double cross! She must have planned to keep the contents of the briefcase all along."

"Then why would his partners think you had the case?"

"I don't know. I think they were grasping at straws when they searched my place, but she has to know where it is. She's the only one who can. I'm not saying she was definitely in on the robbery. Maybe she only found the case after Wayne was murdered and decided to keep the contents for herself. Or maybe she found it and hired someone to kill Wayne so she could keep it."

He rubbed his jaw tiredly. "Sandy, you're upset. You aren't making any sense."

"Of course I'm upset! My daughter's missing and you're too trusting. Zoe Linden *must* have the briefcase. It's the only thing that makes sense. Make her tell you what she did with it!"

"Take it easy."

"They have my daughter!" Her voice caught on a sob. The hysteria drained out of her voice. "She's all I have, Xavier."

He heard her crying and it tore at him.

"She must be so scared."

He gripped the phone, his own chest constricting as he thought of his niece. Was she safe? Had they hurt her? She had to be scared. He was scared for her.

"We're going to find her, Sandy. You have to believe that."

"I know where Harrison is!"

He raised stricken eyes as Zoe appeared in the doorway flushed with excitement. She bit her lip when she realized he was on the phone.

"Sorry."

Sandy had heard her as well. "She's playing you," she shrilled in his ear. "Let me talk to the bitch."

He held up a finger to Zoe to wait and softened his tone. "Sandy, you need to trust me. I'm going to get April back. You have my word."

"But—"

"We're at her fiancé's place right now, going through the things Wayne gave her. I promise you, I'll call you as soon as I have anything at all, okay?"

"Xavier, I'm so scared. I keep thinking of April locked in the dark somewhere and I want to scream."

He swallowed against the tightness at the back of his throat. His eyes stung. Despite his assurances, he feared for his niece as well.

"I know, Sandy. I'll find her. I'll bring her home to you."

He heard her sniff. Her voice was clotted with tears. "Don't trust that woman, Xavier. Please don't trust her."

He looked at Zoe. Her expression held compassion and concern. He wanted to trust her. His instincts said she was telling him the truth, but a little girl's life hung in the balance if he was wrong.

"Trust *me*," he told Sandy softly.

She let out a choked sigh. "It's so hard sitting here waiting."

"I know. Try to rest. I'll call you the minute I learn anything."

"Yes. Please. Anything!"

He disconnected, discouraged and scared. For the millionth time he wondered if he should call the police despite

Sandy's adamant refusal. He understood it. As Wayne's ex-wife her experiences with them had never been pleasant. Guilt by association had automatically made her a suspect in his murder. After all, they had only recently been divorced.

The police had questioned her after Wayne's murder as a matter of course. Sandy didn't have an alibi. She'd been home with April that night. She'd punished April for some misdeed and sent her to her room early, but she couldn't prove it to the men who'd questioned her so aggressively.

Still, the police and the FBI had resources Xavier couldn't begin to match. Surely they would treat her differently as the mother of a missing child. And if April died because of Xavier's ineptitude he wasn't sure he'd be able to live with himself.

"You're worried about your niece."

"I keep wondering if they've hurt her." The words tumbled out as if a dam had been released. "Is she hungry, does she have a place to lie down? She's only seven."

"I'm sorry." Zoe closed the distance between them as he shoved the phone back in its clip.

He swallowed his fear, embarrassed to have revealed so much. "You said you know where your fiancé is?" he asked gruffly.

She nodded, eyes flooded with compassion. "There was a notation on his office calendar. Harrison told me, but I forgot. Artie Van Wheeler was throwing him a bachelor party tonight. Harrison planned to spend the night there because Artie's place is closer to the church."

"You're sure he's there?"

Zoe blinked in surprise. "His wedding tux is gone. So is his overnight bag."

"His wedding tux?"

"Harrison has several tuxedos, but he had one made special for tomorrow. We can be at Artie's place in fifteen minutes at this hour."

"Tell me how to get there."

"I'm coming with you."

"You're safer here."

She looked at him like he'd lost his mind. Maybe he had. Fatigue was starting to take its toll and the evening wasn't over yet.

"Someone just tried to kill us, Xavier. I don't think Harrison will care if we crash his party. Besides, you won't be able to get in without me. Artie has security people who won't let anyone inside without his okay. You do realize it's after one o'clock in the morning. And I am not staying here by myself. You said you were my bodyguard and I'm holding you to it."

"You're the one who said I was your bodyguard." He gazed at the room filled with boxes. "Why don't you call this Artie and talk to Harrison?"

"I already tried. No one is answering the phone. Artie probably had it turned off for the party."

Xavier hesitated. His arm throbbed and there was a headache building over his eyes. Despite his belief that Zoe was honest, Sandy's warning clanged in the back of his head. What if he was wrong? What if Harrison was working with Zoe?

He scraped at the stubble on his chin, feeling foolish for the thought. Harrison Trent owned a penthouse suite. Why would the guy want a stolen briefcase?

Unless he'd hired Wayne to steal it for him.

Xavier's thoughts stumbled over that idea. Trent was the sort of mark his brother liked, not the sort of person who hired someone like Wayne to steal for him. Or was he? Xavier had never known his brother to steal for someone else, but then he hadn't known his brother to take on partners, either. There was always a first time for everything.

"Let's go." If he was walking into a trap, so be it. Any

action at this point was better than standing around. He had to find the briefcase to get April back and every minute he delayed was another minute she suffered.

They didn't speak as they returned to the garage and reclaimed the rental.

Xavier spotted the tail as soon as they hit the street. There was little traffic so he saw the car pulling out the moment he left the parking garage.

"At the risk of upsetting your stomach again, you need to hang on."

Zoe's head swiveled to look behind them. "Someone's following us?"

"Not for long."

Chapter Four

Shaking free of the tail proved a lot simpler than he'd have thought thanks to two police cars at an intersection. Xavier made it through a yellow traffic light, but the car behind them couldn't follow without the cops stopping it for running a red light. Still, Xavier made turn after turn for several minutes before he was fairly certain it was safe to head for the Van Wheeler estate.

Set back from the road and surrounded by stately trees, the Van Wheeler house and grounds were fenced in by tall, spiky wrought-iron while the driveway itself was spanned by a matching gate.

"Oh, no." Zoe stared at the gate.

"What's wrong?"

"It isn't closed all the way."

Xavier stopped the car on the side of the road well short of the entrance. The gate looked closed at first glance, but he saw she was right.

"Maybe they left it open because of the party?" But even as he said it, he felt stirrings of concern.

Zoe bit at her bottom lip. "I suppose it's possible. Harrison's always teasing Artie about his rent-a-cops."

"A guy this rich doesn't have his own security staff?"

"Only Carlton and Leo. They patrol the grounds, monitor the surveillance equipment and hire people when Artie needs extras for parties and special occasions."

"No bodyguards?"

"Ralph fills in when Artie needs one."

"Ralph?"

"His driver. He lives over the front garage and helps with the dogs. Artie has a pair of German shepherds that run loose at night as a rule."

Xavier frowned, studying the scene.

"The security system is tied in to the police department," she continued. "All three men are former marines and ex-cops." Tension and uncertainty underscored her words. "I can't believe the party is still going on this late, but Carlton wouldn't leave the gate open with the dogs out. I don't like this."

Neither did Xavier. "Wait here. I'll check it out."

She was already reaching for her door handle. "Not a chance. If you think I'm going to sit here alone in the dark, think again. Someone already shot you once tonight, and neither of us can shoot back."

Something Xavier was regretting at the moment. And Zoe was right. Although, as a former Navy Seal, Xavier was trained for reconnaissance and could move faster alone, if something was wrong on the grounds, she was safer at his side than sitting helplessly in a car while someone snuck up on her.

"Stay behind me and try not to make any noise."

She slipped from the car, closing the door so quietly it barely made a sound. Xavier turned off the engine and stepped into the night, pausing to listen hard. The usual night sounds filled the air. Even a bat soared across the night sky. Nothing was disturbing the animal and insect life.

Zoe moved to his side and waited. With a frown, Xavier crossed to the gate. There was no telltale light on the mounted camera. Someone had turned off the equipment. His fingers itched for a sidearm. Something *was* wrong.

Slipping past the heavy metal gate, he again paused to listen, letting his eyes sweep the area around them. There were too many trees—too many shadows thrown up by the lights that lined the sweeping, white concrete driveway. Unfortunately, Zoe's peach-colored blouse stood out like a beacon.

If only he had the proper equipment. He didn't like feeling naked when the hair at the back of his neck was prickling a warning like this. Might as well wish for a full unit at his back while he was wishing.

Zoe stayed close as they moved into the tree line. Xavier should have asked if the dogs knew her. He didn't want to come up against a pair of guard-trained German shepherds.

He moved quickly, parallel to the driveway. Zoe stayed with him. For someone without training, she did pretty well, moving with a minimum of excess noise.

The wide driveway curved in a semicircle in front of the main entrance before part of it branched off, sweeping beneath a portico that spanned a two-story double-car garage. The flow of lights flanking the drive moved on to completely surround the sprawling stone house. Mentally, he sighed. Someone had done an excellent job setting up a security perimeter. No one could get near the house without stepping into the light and being caught on the discreetly mounted cameras—when they were working.

Something dark lay sprawled on the concrete halfway between the house and the portico that led to a parking court.

Heart pounding, Xavier paused at the edge of the tree line. Zoe stifled a small sound of distress when she spotted the figure on the drive. She came forward and touched Xavier's arm. "Is that—"

"Quiet," he breathed.

She froze, gaze riveted on the still form.

Xavier assessed the house. Lights glowed in most of the downstairs windows. Only the upstairs was dark—with blank, empty windows capable of hiding potential observers.

"How many people inside?"

Zoe didn't answer. Her gaze was still riveted on the body sprawled on the driveway.

"Zoe? How many staff?"

"Th-three. Callie, the live-in housekeeper. Ralph and the two security men."

He nodded acknowledgment and pointed. In the parking court a black Ferrari was the only car visible. "Harrison's?"

Her head bobbed in agreement. "I think so."

Looked like the party was over, then. Xavier strained to listen for any threat, but the night sounds remained consistent. Whatever had happened to the figure hadn't happened in the past few minutes.

"Do you think he's drunk?"

Xavier shrugged. The front door gaped open in silent, ominous invitation. The hall beyond was lit by an enormous chandelier.

"Dogs?" he asked softly.

"The kennel's behind the second garage on the other side of the parking court. They would have been caged for the party and Carlton would never leave the gate open when he let the dogs loose."

She was assuming the gate had been left open by someone with the authority to leave it open, but Xavier hoped she was right about the dogs. Either they were still caged or they'd already run off. He'd know soon enough. The slight breeze had them upwind of the kennels at the moment, but the minute he went to check on the downed man the animals would have his scent and would set up a clamor.

"Aren't you going to help him?" she whispered.

Xavier studied the house without replying. Nothing stirred behind any of the brightly lit windows. Not only would the dogs scent him, but he'd be an instant target the moment he stepped from the trees. He wasn't anxious to cross that open expanse of concrete. Common sense demanded he get Zoe out of there and summon help.

"We need to go."

"No!"

"Quiet! We'll call for help."

"Harrison's in there."

She was going to be stubborn. And what would happen to April if he brought the police and FBI into this now? But if he didn't, he had a feeling Zoe wasn't going to like what they found inside. He didn't think the man lying there was drunk.

He took her face, forcing her gaze to meet his. "Wait here." He pressed a finger over lips that formed an immediate protest. Her eyes widened. He handed her the car keys. Her skin was icy despite the warmth of the evening. "Anything happens, anything at all, get to the car and call the police." He thrust his cell phone in her hand as well. "Understand me?"

"You're going inside."

"Zoe. Do you understand?"

Her eyes snapped with anger. *Good.* Anger was better than shock, and he didn't think she was far from that state now.

"Yes."

"Be ready to run."

She swore, surprising him. "Don't you *dare* get killed."

Xavier stroked her shoulder, offering the only reassurance he could. Then he was moving, running as he'd been trained. His body tensed for a bullet that never came.

It seemed anticlimactic when he reached the victim. The tuxedo-clad man didn't stir when touched. In the distance, as expected, the dogs began to bark. It didn't sound as if they were drawing closer so they probably were still caged. He crouched over the man, feeling for a pulse.

Finding one, he sent a nod toward the woods to indicate the man was alive. There were no visible signs of blood or trauma. The victim could have been stabbed or shot and bleeding internally or he could be stunned or drugged. He didn't smell drunk. Xavier scowled. There wasn't time to check and not much he could do if he found any wounds, given the situation.

An earpiece in the man's ear told Xavier this was one of the security people. The baton, pepper spray, Taser and flashlight were confirmation. Relieving the man of all four, Xavier stood. The dogs continued to sound the alarm.

Zoe ran over as he rose to his feet.

"I told you to wait!"

She glared right back. "You nodded."

A poor excuse and she knew it.

"And now you have a gun."

"It's a Taser, not a gun."

"At least it's a weapon. Is he all right?" She looked down at the man on the pavement. "That's Carlton. He's one of the security guards."

"He's breathing. Come on."

"We can't just leave him here!"

"You want to carry him?" Without waiting, he led the way to the open front door. There was no point trying to send her back to the woods. Anyone inside the house now knew they had company.

The house was new construction with soaring ceilings and expansive rooms. An overhead bridge spanned the living room and the foyer. His neck prickled against impending attack from someone lurking up there in the dark. Fingers curled over the pepper spray. He didn't like this. The house was too quiet and too open. An attack could come from any direction. The pepper spray was his only distance weapon.

He motioned for Zoe to wait. She shook her head. Scowling, he began moving quickly from room to room to clear the ground floor. They found the second body in the kitchen. A woman's foot sticking out from behind the counter caused Zoe to inhale sharply.

Xavier motioned her to stay put and inched forward. A coffee cup lay a few feet from the woman's outstretched hand. The contents had splashed across the floor and lower cupboards. Like the man out front, the woman was dressed in a tuxedo.

"Breathing," he told Zoe in a whisper. And again, no sign of a wound.

"We can't just leave her here."

He didn't bother to reply. After a second's hesitation Zoe followed him as he moved into what was obviously the party room.

Extra chairs and small tables were scattered about. Odd-looking balloons bobbed eerily. A closer look proved they were inflated condoms. He should have guessed, given the sexual nature of the streamers and signs hung everywhere.

After a startled breath, Zoe wouldn't meet his gaze. He was mildly embarrassed as well when he saw the melting ice sculptures on the polished bar. Even distorted, there was little doubt of what they portrayed.

Mingled scents of alcohol, perfume, aftershave and food clung to the air. Glasses, some still half-full, empty plates and plates with half-eaten cake sat amid table decorations he chose not to examine.

Zoe squirmed uncomfortably. He followed her line of sight to a long feather tassel obscenely clinging to what appeared to be a woman's pastie on the floor.

The rest of the downstairs proved empty, including an enormous master bedroom suite. The bed hadn't been used. However, a tie and cummerbund had been tossed on a dresser beside an expensive pair of emerald-and-gold cuff links. Xavier expected to find Van Wheeler's body in the master bath or closet. It was unsettling to find both empty.

His senses were alert to the slightest sound. Every minute they spent inside this house increased the danger that someone would discover them there. He didn't think whoever had taken out the guard and the woman was still inside, but people often died making foolish assumptions.

"Guest rooms are upstairs," she told him quietly. "Harrison always uses the first room off the main staircase."

"We'll take the back stairs. I want you to wait at the top of the stairs while I clear the rooms first. If anything happens you get out of here. Are we clear?"

Relieved by her nod, he headed for the rear staircase near the service porch. A glance outside at the parking court confirmed that the only car was the black Ferrari, sitting in full view. The dogs had fallen silent. Xavier wasn't sure if that was good or bad.

With the pepper spray gripped tightly in one hand and the flashlight in the other, he searched each room before crossing the bridge that overlooked the foyer and living room.

Every room was dark, every door open. Not until he approached the one Zoe had told him Trent liked to use did he find the first trace of occupancy. The bedding wasn't just rumpled. The blanket and sheet were on the floor. So were a lamp and a clock radio. Obviously, there had been a struggle.

Pulse racing, he sent the flashlight beam about the room. A wallet and cell phone sat on the dresser. An overnight case rested open on the floor.

The tuxedo hanging in the closet and the case of men's toiletries on the sink of the huge bathroom that connected with an adjoining bedroom confirmed that Harrison had been there. But he wasn't there now. The connecting bedroom was pristine, with a neatly made bed.

Xavier stepped into the hall and motioned to Zoe. She ran to join him, and he flashed the beam about the room, stopping it on the wallet and cell phone. "Harrison's?"

She started forward. When she would have reached for them he shook his head in warning. Something crunched under his foot as he took a step back. The flashlight beam picked up the broken remnants of a syringe.

He caught his breath. Mentally, he cursed. He could almost taste her fear as she saw what he had stepped on. He kept his voice to a whisper. "Does Trent use drugs?"

"No! Of course not."

"You sure?"

"Yes."

But her tone waffled. She was smart enough to know there was always a possibility. All kinds of good people had dirty little secrets. Trent obviously had the sort of money to keep a drug habit well concealed. However, given what they'd found, Xavier didn't think that was the case.

The implication behind the syringe wasn't one he liked any better than she did. His thoughts flashed to April. Were they keeping her drugged? Would it permanently harm her?

What had his brother stolen that could warrant kidnapping two millionaires and a little girl?

"They took him, didn't they?" Zoe whispered.

"I don't know. We have at least four people unaccounted for, including Trent and Van Wheeler." He led her out of the room and over to the main staircase. "Based on the syringe and the fact that the two people we found are breathing, I'd say this was an inside job and they were drugged instead of being killed." And that boded well for April.

They reached the foyer. He paused to survey the scene outside. Nothing had changed.

"There's a basement," she told him.

He stepped into the study off the foyer. "We'll let the police check it out. We need to go."

Her eyes widened. He used the hem of his shirt to lift the telephone on the desk. "Who are you calling?"

"911. Just because they've been drugged doesn't mean they might not die from whatever was used. The minute I disconnect we're going to run straight down the driveway to the car. Don't stop for any reason at all."

Now he wished he hadn't left the rental car on the road. The street wasn't highly traveled, but someone could have noticed it and noted the license plate. The car would trace right back to him.

Careful not to leave any fingerprints, Xavier dialed 911 with a knuckle.

"Fire, ambulance or police?"

"There's something's wrong at the Van Wheeler place," he told the operator. "You'd better send help."

He hung up as she began to question him. "Go!"

Zoe turned and ran. Xavier followed, hoping there wasn't a police unit in the immediate vicinity.

Luck was with them. They didn't pass another car until they were close to the highway.

"Where are we going?"

He slanted a glance at Zoe as they passed under a streetlight. She looked as exhausted as he felt. "Any suggestions?"

"I can't think." She closed her eyes and opened them again. "Someplace with a bed. I can barely keep my eyes open. Why would Wayne's partners kidnap Harrison?"

"Good question."

He wished he knew for sure what was going on behind

those stricken features. Was she involved or an innocent by-stander? Was Trent connected to the theft somehow?

Too many possibilities and not enough information. Xavier scrubbed his jaw with a tired hand. He didn't care what was in the briefcase or who wanted it. All he wanted was April back safe and unharmed. "There's a motel up ahead."

"Fine. I don't care. They took him because of me, didn't they?"

Instead of answering, he touched her hand lightly where it rested on her thigh. Her fingers were cold. Minutes later he left her sitting in the car with her eyes closed while he went into the motel and registered.

He wanted a pair of adjoining rooms, but all they had left at this hour was a single with a queen-size bed on the third floor. The night was more than half over and they both needed sleep. Xavier didn't quibble. When he returned to the car Zoe was sound asleep. He wasn't sure whether to be alarmed or relieved. Emotions surfaced that he hadn't felt for a woman in a long time. Long lashes lay against her pale cheeks, bringing a deep surge of protective instincts on his part. Being a strongly independent woman, she probably wouldn't thank him.

And she was pregnant. She didn't look pregnant, he decided once more. She looked soft and vulnerable and un-bearably lovely. He swore under his breath.

She barely came awake when he roused her to explain the situation. He didn't think she even heard his offer to sleep on the floor. She followed him blindly, more asleep than awake as they took the elevator to the second floor, where she stumbled into the room, kicked off her shoes and used the bathroom before sliding into the bed fully dressed. She was asleep before her head hit the pillow.

His sister Lorraine had been that way when she was pregnant, all energy until she crashed and burned. Xavier looked at Zoe's sleeping features, troubled by his overwhelming desire to protect her.

He kicked off his shoes and sat in the desk chair for long minutes, watching her sleep. Delicate features masked an iron will and an intelligence he was coming to admire. Xavier liked the way she'd handled herself tonight. She'd kept her head in an emergency and she had followed directions. As long as she'd agreed with them, he mused wryly.

It was hard not to envy Harrison Trent.

Looking at the wide expanse of bed beside Zoe, he gave in to his own exhaustion and lay down beside her on top of the covers. He wasn't going to do April any good if he collapsed. Zoe would never know. It seemed a waste not to put all that inviting soft space to good use. He'd just rest for a couple of minutes.

Sandy might believe Zoe was involved in his brother's murder, but every instinct he had said Sandy was wrong. Zoe was exactly what she appeared to be—a woman who'd gotten mixed up with the wrong man. Xavier knew exactly how easy that was where his brother was concerned.

He turned off the light and lay back, dismissing the memory of his own engagement with an ease that gave him pause. Probing the old wound, he discovered the memory no longer hurt. Wayne had done them both a favor in the long run when he'd taken Xavier's fiancée to bed.

While Kath had been hurt when she'd discovered it had been a game for Wayne, who'd had no intention of replacing Xavier at the altar, the brief affair had helped her discover that she wanted a very different lifestyle from the one Xavier had been offering. A year later she'd found herself a wealthy stockbroker. The last he'd heard the two had moved to New York City, where she had settled happily. It had hurt at the time. He wasn't sure when he'd come to realize how wrong their marriage would have been. He only wished he'd had a chance to tell Wayne he'd done Xavier a favor in the long run.

Not that Wayne would have cared. Wayne had gone his own way in all things, discarding people as easily as changing clothes. Xavier didn't think Sandy had ever come to terms with that. She'd lasted far longer than most women in his brother's life, probably because of April. Whatever else his brother had been, he'd cared about his daughter. And Xavier was pretty sure Sandy still loved Wayne. Most of his women did.

Did Zoe?

Chapter Five

Zoe was still sleeping when Xavier woke to find his arm curved protectively around her. She slept curled against him, spoon fashioned. It had been some time since he'd woken with a woman in his bed, and Xavier was surprised by how natural it felt with Zoe.

He lay still for several minutes, savoring the sensation. She breathed easily, deeply asleep. Impulsively, he kissed her hair, then quietly slipped from the bed before he gave in to the growing desire to do far more than that. The heavy drapes covering the window blocked any vestiges of daylight, inviting deep sleep. If it hadn't been for the noises coming from the hall outside, he might still be asleep, too.

Moving to the bathroom, Xavier studied the stubble on his chin and decided, at the very least, that a quick shower was mandated.

Zoe still hadn't moved when he left the room and headed for the front desk. The helpful clerks dug out a disposable razor, toothpaste, a pair of toothbrushes and even a comb for Zoe. The tiny gift shop wasn't open and didn't run to clothing anyhow, but they did have a coffee shop that served breakfast until noon. Eyeing the food, he called his sister.

"Talk to me about morning sickness," he asked when he got Lorraine on the phone. The pause lasted several beats.

"At eight o'clock in the morning. Why?"

"I need to know how to help someone."

"Sandy's pregnant?"

"No."

"Okay, April's only seven, so what's going on?"

The mention of his niece twisted his insides. "Lorraine, I don't have time. There's a pregnant woman who will be waking up any time now. Based on last night, she'll start being sick as soon as she opens her eyes. Didn't Bill bring you toast or something every morning?"

"Soda crackers and ginger ale. And you know this conversation requires a detailed explanation."

He knew. "Later."

"Soda crackers and ginger ale work best, but failing that, dry toast and cola or sweet tea. It depends on the person. Have her eat some before she actually gets up. Then she should lay there for about fifteen minutes to let her stomach settle. Does she have a name?"

"Yes."

"You are so going to get it when I see you."

"No doubt."

"Are you bringing her with April?"

He closed his eyes for a second against the flash of pain. "No."

"But you *are* bringing April home?"

As soon as he found her. He hadn't told anyone about her kidnapping because the last thing he wanted was his entire family charging up here to help. And they would have done, down to the youngest member.

"Eventually, yes. Is there anything else I should know?"

"It would fill an encyclopedia, but for your immediate purposes, she should drink small amounts of fluids during the day so she doesn't dehydrate, avoid strong smells, especially strong food smells, and no coffee."

"So bacon and eggs are out."

"Ugh. Absolutely. Scrambled eggs maybe later if she feels up to them. Tell me one thing. Is this your baby?"

The thought caused a pang of longing. He'd always wanted kids. "In less than a week? Hardly."

"Let me talk to April."

If only she could. He gritted his teeth. "We've got a situation here, sis." And he was wasting precious time when every minute might count. "I'll get back to you as soon as I can. For now, don't say anything to Mom or the others, all right?"

"What would I say?"

"Thanks. I owe you."

"So many times I've lost count. Call me when you can."

"Will do."

The woman behind the food counter was sympathetic when he explained his "wife's" plight. He waited impatiently while she located packets of soda crackers and a can of ginger ale. It wasn't cold, but she added ice to a glass. Regretfully, he skipped his morning coffee and headed back to the room.

ZOE OPENED HER EYES and stared at the ceiling, disoriented. This wasn't her bedroom. It wasn't even the bedroom at the condo. Noises in the hall outside the room put it all in perspective, and the events of the night before came rushing in.

An image of the broken syringe, the lamp and clock radio and the bed with its sheet and blanket strewn across the floor sent her pulse racing. What had happened to Harrison? Where were he and Artie? Artie was so security conscious, how could they be missing?

Come to that, where was Xavier? Her eyes skimmed the

room. The pillow beside her showed a depression. He'd slept on the bed next to her? A tingle went through her at the thought.

Was she losing her mind? No tingles! She was getting married that morning. She had no business feeling this strong pull of attraction to someone she'd just met, no matter how sexy he was. And Wayne's brother, no less!

Hormones. They were going crazy and so was she.

Her hand went to her stomach. It was definitely rounded even if she wasn't showing as much as she thought she should be by now. The doctor kept telling her everyone was different. She and the baby were fine. While she believed him, it frightened her to think a child was growing inside her. What if something *was* wrong? What if she made a horrible mother?

A human life would depend on her for years to come. It was an awesome responsibility.

She shied from that thought as she tugged at her blouse, where it had bunched at her back. She'd slept in her clothes. She'd never done that before. They were undoubtedly rumpled beyond repair, but she had nothing else to wear. Hopefully, the motel had an iron.

The thought of explaining this situation to Harrison made her cringe. And that was stupid. She should be more worried that she wouldn't get the chance to explain the situation to him. Was he even all right?

She eyed her purse on the desk across the room and willed her cell phone to ring. Let him call and tell her he was fine.

Her bladder began its insistent demands. How could something as small as a four-month-old fetus put pressure on her bladder? She stroked her tummy lovingly, but before she could rise, the sound of someone at the door sent fear slamming through her. The door opened even as she tried to disentangle herself from the blanket and sheet. Xavier strode inside, carrying a tray.

"Stay right there. My sister said this will help."

"What?"

"Morning sickness." He set several packages of soda crackers on the nightstand and opened a can of ginger ale, pouring some over ice in a glass also on the tray.

The sound was the final catalyst. Zoe swung out of bed. "I don't have morning sickness. I have to pee. Get out of my way!" She nearly knocked him over rushing for the bathroom.

"But you aren't supposed to get up until after you eat the crackers," he called through the closed door.

She was so embarrassed. The minute she finished washing her hands she flung open the door to glare at him. "Tell me you did not tell your sister about me."

He backed up a space and held up his hands. "Not specifics. I just called her for some advice."

"About me!"

"About morning sickness. She has three munchkins of her own so I figured she qualified as an expert. I remembered her husband always got up and brought her something first thing in the morning."

The love in his voice when he referred to his sister made her suddenly feel terribly alone.

"Did you tell her you slept with me?"

For a second, surprise left him speechless. He cocked his head, studying her expression. The tension left his shoulders. He rocked back on his heels with a decidedly wicked twinkle in his eye. "I'm not that kind of guy."

How dare he tease her! He had no right to look so sexy first thing in the morning. And since when did she find morning stubble sexy?

Zoe grimaced, shutting her eyes. What was she thinking? She opened them again to find him gesturing at the rumpled sheets. "It's a big bed, Zoe. You weren't supposed to notice."

"You're what, six-two?"

"Six-one."

"Oh, well, then, that makes you easy to overlook. Therefore you can explain last night to Harrison."

"There's nothing to explain."

"*I* know that. Harrison won't."

His lips quirked. "Does he own a gun?"

He was teasing her again. "I hope so." She eyed the ginger ale and crackers as her stomach rumbled. "If you really want to help me, crackers aren't going to cut it."

"But Lorraine said—"

"Steak. Rare."

His eyes widened. "That's not even safe."

"You're a nutritionist now?" She ripped the cellophane from a packet of crackers with her teeth, aware of his bemused expression. "I need iron and protein. And peanut butter."

"Peanut butter?"

"Peanut butter," she agreed firmly, chewing and swallowing the first cracker. She made a face at the dryness and took a swallow of the ginger ale. "Didn't they have any crackers with peanut butter downstairs?" She ate the second cracker while he continued staring at her.

"They serve only a light breakfast downstairs," he finally managed.

"No peanut butter?"

"It's not a regular restaurant."

"Is there one close by? I'm starving."

"But my sister said—"

"Peanut butter," she reiterated firmly. "And steak, but really, really rare. I'm not kidding. While you're gone I'll take a quick shower. I don't suppose this motel has a clothing boutique?"

"No."

"Okay. What time is it?"

"Eight twenty-three."

"Oh, no! We have to get moving! I need to be at the church by ten-thirty. We have to stop and pick up my dress and my shoes."

"Zoe—"

She didn't want to hear what he was about to say. "Hurry with the steak. And don't forget the peanut butter."

Grabbing the rest of the crackers and the glass of ginger ale, she tore past him back into the bathroom. She could not be late for her own wedding even if the groom wasn't going to show.

What if he did?

Her heart hammered against her chest. She'd get married, of course. "But I don't want to marry Harrison," she told her wide-eyed reflection softly.

There. She'd said it out loud. He was her boss and her friend—a very dear, good friend. She didn't want that to change. She didn't want to be his wife.

"Oh, God." Marriage had seemed so reasonable when Harrison had proposed the idea.

She was pregnant and alone and someone was trying to kill her. The police had admitted they couldn't do much to protect her after someone tried to shoot her the first time. It had happened shortly after she and Wayne had broken up.

She and Harrison and Artie had been leaving work one evening when someone had started shooting. Harrison had knocked her down and thrown himself over her. It was a miracle that neither of them had been hit. Wayne hadn't been as lucky when the killer had tried again. He'd died because he'd had the misfortune to be standing right next to her. And she still had no idea why someone was coming after her.

The police had gone back over the airplane accident that had killed her parents and her brother three years earlier, looking for a possible connection but had found nothing.

Harrison had hired his own security people to investigate a possible work-related cause, but they hadn't come up with anything, either. Then Wayne had been killed and the police had told her about his past.

Harrison felt guilty that she'd met Wayne at his party. Not that it had been his fault. Harrison hadn't invited Wayne. Nor could he have known Wayne would turn his incredible charm on Zoe. And none of that explained why she had become a target.

Because she had no close family to turn to, Harrison's support meant everything. Right after the first attempt, he'd brought in Carter Hughes and had the attorney run interference with the police and the media. Zoe had always been an independent person, but nightmares and bouts of nausea had left her weepy and afraid. She had been barely functional at work, tiring quickly. Harrison had insisted she see a doctor.

It had almost been a relief to learn her mood swings, the nausea and tiredness were all symptoms of an unplanned pregnancy even though they had used protection.

Harrison had held her when her emotions had shattered at the news, overwhelming her with the idea of being a mother. Harrison was her boss, her friend, her mentor. He could make anything sound reasonable. So when he'd insisted he would protect her and offered to give her unborn child a father and a shot at the sort of home life she longed to recapture, she'd found herself going along with the plan.

She loved Harrison. She just wasn't in love with him.

He'd told her that didn't matter. He wasn't in love with her, either, but they would make it work. They worked well together and there was no reason to think they couldn't carry that over into a shared life. He was tired of the dating scene and certain he was never going to meet anyone who saw him as more than a wealthy acquisition.

She should have put up more of a protest, because once he

thought they were in agreement, he'd hired a wedding planner and had set a date. Everything snowballed so fast from there, Zoe had had little time for doubts.

"And I didn't want doubts," she told her reflection. "I wanted what my parents had. So I ignored everything and took the easy way." Only, that morning, her doubts threatened to swallow her whole.

What if Harrison met someone after they married?

What if she did?

Blinking back sudden tears, Zoe mentally cursed her crazy hormones. She had only a couple of hours to get her wedding gown, make herself a presentable bride and show up at the church. She was getting married at eleven o'clock.

If the groom showed up.

If Wayne's killers didn't murder her first.

"PEANUT BUTTER?" THE perplexed desk clerks stared at Xavier as if he were insane. "Um, there's a convenience store down the street where you could probably buy some."

"And there's a pancake place a few doors past that," the other clerk put in. "They probably serve steak and eggs for breakfast."

"Thanks."

Peanut butter. Xavier shook his head. Lorraine hadn't mentioned cravings, although Xavier did recall Bill saying he'd bought so much butter pecan ice cream with her third pregnancy that he should have owned stock in the company.

But peanut butter and rare steak?

What did it matter? The sooner he fed Zoe, the sooner they could get moving. Xavier drove to the restaurant to place the carryout order, troubled by his chaotic thoughts. Would anyone feed April this morning?

That way lay madness so he steered away from the thought. He had to stay focused on the task, not on the victim. He'd feed Zoe and grill her about any possible places Wayne might have mentioned. The briefcase had to be somewhere. And he would not think about how incredibly appealing Zoe had looked that morning, all tousled and rumpled from sleep.

What was wrong with him? The only thing that mattered right now was April. He saw bikini-clad women daily without feeling this disturbing pull of attraction.

Too much stress and too little sleep. He needed to pull himself together and stay focused.

Xavier drove to the convenience mart and picked up a large jar of peanut butter. After a moment's consideration he added peanut butter crackers, peanut butter cookies, a case of bottled water, some plastic silverware and a few other possible "essentials" before returning to get Zoe's steak and the meal he'd ordered for himself.

Zoe was just exiting the steamy bathroom when he returned. The scent of soap and shampoo drifted out with her. Her hair was still slightly damp on the ends and her cheeks were filled with color. She'd ironed her shirt and slacks and looked calm, professional and aloof. He preferred her as he'd seen her earlier, fresh from the bed. He shoved that thought aside and set about taking out the food containers.

Watching her slather peanut butter on the rare slab of meat a few minutes later, however, made him want to gag.

"What's the matter?" she demanded.

"I've never seen anyone do that before."

"Think of it as steak sauce, only thicker."

Xavier tried not to shudder. The scent of peanut butter overwhelmed the small room.

"Aren't you hungry?" she asked.

"Not anymore."

She cut into the bleeding steak with relish. "As soon as I finish eating I'm going to call Artie's house."

He nodded and tried not to watch as she stirred peanut butter into the helpless scrambled eggs before slathering more on a slice of toast.

"There was nothing on the radio about last night," he informed her before taking a bite of his own food.

"What does that mean?"

"That someone's clamped a media lid on what happened."

"That's a good thing, right?"

"Yes." Fascinated despite himself, he ate absently, watching her eat with dainty precision and a speed that would do a truck driver proud. Maybe he should have ordered her a second steak.

"Who did it?" she asked.

"Clamp down on the media?" Xavier shrugged. "The police, a relative—"

"Harrison or Artie! They could be back. Maybe it wasn't what it looked like. Maybe it was a robbery that happened after they were already gone."

He didn't bother correcting her. She didn't believe a word of it, either. She spread more peanut butter on her toast but set it aside. She reached for the telephone on the desk and punched in a string of numbers. Her fingers trembled when she set the receiver back down minutes later.

"Artie's line is busy. That's a good sign, isn't it?"

He had no idea. "Try again in a few minutes."

Zoe nodded. Xavier was being so nice. He could have dumped her last night when he'd realized she didn't know where the missing briefcase was. His goal was to find his niece. Remembering the genuine anguish in his voice when he'd spoken of her, Zoe knew that was one of the reasons she was drawn to him.

"I know it's probably pointless, but I'll try Harrison's cell again," she told him.

She shoved aside the remains of her meal, and Xavier began cleaning up while she dialed. Harrison's cell phone rang straight to voice mail. The phone was probably still sitting on the dresser in Artie's spare room.

Renewed fear made her stomach lurch. "They really kidnapped him, didn't they?"

Xavier's silence was confirmation.

Zoe punched in Artie's number once more. This time the phone was answered immediately.

"Artie?"

"Zoe? Thank God! Where are you? I've been trying to call you all morning."

"I'm—"

"Something's happened. It's bad, Zoe."

Fear paralyzed her.

"The police are here. They want to talk to you."

"Artie, what happened?"

He swore softly. "Sorry. There's no good way to say this. Harrison's gone, Zoe. Someone hit my place last night after the party. They got in, drugged the staff and went after Harrison."

She tried not to think about Callie on the kitchen floor or Carlton crumpled on the hard cement of the driveway. "Is everyone okay?"

"I don't know yet."

He sucked in a ragged breath. Zoe pictured him running thick fingers through his thinning hair.

"They took everyone to the hospital. The bastards got onto the grounds somehow, dismantled the cameras and drugged everyone. The dogs were still locked up. I'm sorry, Zoe. It looks like Harrison was the target. He put up a struggle, but someone snatched him. Nothing else was touched as far as I can determine."

She bit her lip. Until then, she'd held on to a trace of hope that maybe what they'd seen last night had been something other than what it looked like.

"I know what you're thinking, Zoe, but this probably has nothing to do with you. Harrison's always been a target, you know that. He's rich and powerful so don't start blaming yourself. This isn't your fault."

"Unless it is," she told him softly.

He swore again. "The police want to talk with you," he repeated. "You don't have to worry, Carter Hughes is here. He won't let them bully you."

She ignored the mention of the lawyer. "Where were you last night, Artie?"

Tension vied with exhaustion in his voice. "My sister showed up after the party. You remember Sybil?"

"Yes. Of course."

"Her son Tad and some of his friends got arrested last night. It's a long story, but his father's in Germany so Sybil came here because she didn't know what else to do. She tried to call me but I'd turned off the phones because of the party. You know me."

Zoe did. Artie did business all over the world. It wasn't unusual for him to get phone calls at all hours of the day or night, so he frequently turned off his phones when he had guests.

"I don't know how Sybil drove all the way over here without wrecking. She was so upset. I had to get her calmed down before I could even call Carter. Then I had to arrange bail and we had to go to the police station in Potomac to get the kid. It was so late by then I figured I wouldn't bother asking Ralph to drive us."

His brittle laugh was more of a choking sound.

"Ralph was parking cars all night for the party so I figured he'd earned his rest. I had no idea he was in his room over the garage unconscious."

He sucked in a deep, steadying breath. He treated his staff like friends. Zoe knew he was taking this hard.

"Harrison had already gone upstairs for the night when Sybil arrived. When I got her calmed down I just called out to Callie to tell her we were leaving. She was probably already unconscious and I didn't have a clue."

Anger, frustration and guilt filled his voice, but he kept control. "I drove Sybil's car to the police station. By the time I got back here early this morning, there were cops and ambulances everywhere. We spent all morning working on rumor control but it's a mess. Zoe, please tell me you've heard from Harrison. Tell me he just got cold feet and left before all hell broke loose."

Her heart was leaden. "I haven't heard from him."

"God, kid, you'd better get over here."

"Yes. I'm on my way."

"I'm so damn sorry."

"Artie, do you think Carter could call the wedding planner? We need to cancel the service right away."

Artie swore. Zoe swallowed hard. "I'd do it myself but I don't even know what to tell people."

"Me, either. I'm sorry, Zoe," he repeated. "I'll have Carter call. It's Maureen Arquette, right?"

"Yes."

"Are you okay? The baby?"

"I'm fine. We're both fine." She was aware that Xavier watched her impatiently with narrowed eyes. "Artie, I have to go. I'll be there shortly."

"Zoe, be careful. You've got that bodyguard Harrison hired, right?"

She raised her eyes to meet Xavier's. "I have a bodyguard right here with me."

"Good. Don't take any chances."

"I won't. You stay safe, too," she ordered before hanging up.

"Let's go," Xavier demanded as soon as she disconnected.

"Artie says the police want to talk to me."

"No."

The flatness in his voice chilled her. "What do you mean, no?"

"You can't talk to the police. Not yet."

She stood to face him, angry and scared to her soul. She couldn't stop shaking inside. "They've got your niece, Xavier. Now they have Harrison. We need police help."

"And what do you think they're going to do with April and Harrison once these men know the police are involved?"

Her breath caught in her lungs. They'd killed Wayne and tried to kill her. They weren't going to care if they killed a millionaire and a seven-year-old child as well.

"If we go to the police the media will pick up the story. They'll kill both of them, Zoe. You know I'm right."

She knew.

"Let's go."

"Where?"

He didn't answer. He lifted the bag of groceries he'd brought inside, picked up his suitcase and set the room key on the dresser. Then he grabbed her arm.

Suddenly it was all too much. Overwhelmed by too many emotions, Zoe planted her feet. "If you don't want me to kick something sensitive, you'll let go of my arm right now."

Surprise flickered in his dark eyes, but he released her and waited. She was cold all over. "I don't like being manhandled." She strode past him and reached for the door.

"I'm sorry, Zoe."

She nodded but didn't turn around. "So am I. Where are we going?"

He exhaled on a sigh. "To see April's mother." He opened the door and followed her down the hall.

April's mother. Wayne's ex-wife. "Why?"

"Wayne's partners are supposed to get in touch with her. They want to trade April."

"For me."

"For the briefcase."

"Which we don't have."

"If the three of us put our heads together maybe we can come up with something. Who's Carter?"

"Carter Hughes is an attorney and a friend of Harrison's and Artie's. I thought he handled only contract law but I guess not." As they rode the empty elevator down to the lobby she told him what Artie had said.

"And Van Wheeler said they're keeping a lid on things?"

"He called it rumor control."

"He can call it duck soup as long as Harrison's kidnapping doesn't hit the media. I don't want these guys getting any more spooked than they already are."

Zoe shuddered as the doors opened. Xavier led the way to the side entrance leading into the parking area. Remembering what had happened last night, she remained silent and alert at his side as they sprinted for the rental car. He tossed his suitcase in the trunk. Not until they were inside with the doors locked and the engine running did Xavier continue their conversation.

"It isn't going to take the police long to connect what happened at your condo with what happened at Van Wheeler's place."

She latched her seat belt as he pulled out of the parking space.

"I didn't think about that. But if I don't talk to the police right away, won't they think something happened to me as well? They might even think I had something to do with what happened to Harrison."

"At the moment," he told her, "the police are the least of your worries."

Xavier risked a glance in her direction. Calm concern filled her expression, but he knew it was a sham. She was as scared as he was.

"Turn left at the next intersection," she told him.

"Why?"

"The church is that direction."

His stomach clenched. "No way." He met her gaze as he stopped for a red light. She looked serious and determined.

"Zoe, the church is the first place they'll look for you."

"That can't be helped. If Harrison gets free that's where he'll go."

"Trent isn't stupid, Zoe. If your fiancé gets free he'll go to the cops. Wayne's partners don't want him, they want you."

"Which is why Harrison will go to the church. He'll try to protect me. You don't have to come, but I have to go there, Xavier."

Her mulish expression was firm.

"Zoe, he isn't going to show."

She didn't respond.

"And what do we do when Wayne's partners start shooting at us?"

"Drive like the wind?"

She wasn't smiling. Her fingers were curled in fists around her purse.

"I still say it's a poor bodyguard who doesn't carry a gun."

"I'm not a bodyguard, remember?"

"You've done a terrific job so far."

He couldn't think of a response to that. He did want to protect her. Zoe was another of Wayne's casualties.

"I never thanked you for last night," she added. "Thank you."

"You're welcome." His gruff tone didn't put her off.

"Maybe you're in the wrong profession, Xavier."

"No," he told her firmly. "I'm not."

She blinked and gripped her purse even more tightly. "Look, I know Harrison isn't likely to show up, but you must see that I have to go there to be sure. There could be another explanation for what we saw at Artie's."

"Name one."

When she didn't respond he sighed audibly. "It's too big a risk." Yet he was still heading in the direction she'd indicated.

"You don't have to go with me."

"They have my niece," he reminded her flatly.

"I'm sorry, Xavier. I know you're worried about her. So am I. If we could spot one of those men without being seen, maybe we could follow him back to where they're holding her."

"You're stretching."

"I know, but it's all I've got."

And this was a battle he wasn't going to win. "I'll drive past the church, but we're not getting out of the car."

"Unless we see Harrison."

"Unless I tell you it's safe," he corrected. "I mean it, Zoe. Do we have a deal?"

"Yes." She scowled, but leaned forward in the seat. "Take that next street on the left. The church is two blocks up on our right."

"Okay, but stay low in your seat while I circle the block."

Zoe's pulse quickened. She should have been going inside about now to get ready to walk down the aisle. This should have been the happiest day of her life. Instead she felt guilty and sad and afraid.

And relieved.

She closed her eyes, but the thought wouldn't go away. As they drove past, her maid of honor was holding a dress bag and climbing the stone steps to the church. Zoe winced. She hadn't even called Helen or the other members of the wedding party. She should have. Her friends deserved to hear an explanation from her, not the wedding planner. She started to reach inside her purse for her cell phone and stopped. What could she possibly say to them?

Xavier turned down a side street. A car in front of them braked suddenly as a pedestrian darted across the road. Traffic came to an abrupt standstill in both directions. Zoe's gaze landed on the car approaching from the opposite side of the road. The striking brunette woman behind the wheel was pointing to the roof of the building across the street from the front of the church. But it was the man beside her, leaning forward to follow the direction of her finger that unhinged Zoe's jaw.

"Harrison! That's Harrison!"

Chapter Six

Xavier barely heard her as he swore. "Hang on," he ordered. As traffic opened slightly he sped forward and whipped the car around the nearest corner.

"What are you doing? You're going the wrong way! That's Harrison back there. Turn around!"

"The guy from the parking lot last night is in a dark-green sedan right behind us."

"What?"

He swore again as the sedan broke free of traffic and sped to catch up. "Get down in case he starts shooting."

"But Harrison's back there!"

"Then he better hope he isn't spotted. Get down!" He yanked on her arm, driving as fast as he dared trying to place as much distance between them and the sedan as possible. "I saw the guy in his car when traffic stopped for that pedestrian back there. He was parked on the side of the road watching the church."

I told you so was implied. "He nearly caused an accident pulling out when he saw us go past."

"But what about Harrison?"

Keeping a close eye on the sedan, Xavier wove in and out of traffic. "You're sure it was your fiancé you saw?"

"Yes!"

"Did he see you?"

Her voice flattened. "I don't know. I don't think so. He was looking at something the woman was pointing out."

"What woman?"

"She was driving the car. I've never seen her before."

Remembering the pastie from the night before, the bedroom struggle suddenly took on a whole new perspective. Sex and drugs? Could it be that simple?

No. Not when the staff had been drugged as well.

"Did Trent look like he was in trouble?"

"No."

Her tone was distressed, but Xavier didn't have time to worry about her fiancé at the moment. Traffic was heavy and the area was unfamiliar. On a positive note, the other cars on the road were keeping the sedan from drawing any closer for the moment. Both of them were now hemmed in.

If the goal was to take Zoe alive to ask her about the briefcase, Xavier figured the driver wouldn't start firing without a clear shot.

"Was anyone else in the car?"

"I didn't see anyone, but I only had a glimpse before we passed them. We need to turn around and go back."

"And then what?" They were already several blocks from the church.

Zoe didn't answer. Xavier's attention was split between the traffic in front and the green car behind. An opening came for the other driver to move forward, but he didn't. Xavier frowned. Why was he hanging back? He must know Xavier had seen him.

"Is he still behind us?"

"Yes. Don't turn around."

"I'm not stupid, Xavier. What's he doing?"

"Nothing. I suspect he's waiting for a better opportunity. I think we should give him one."

"What?"

As they stopped for another traffic light, he studied the buildings lining the street. "Are you familiar with this area?"

"Yes. My obstetrician has an office in a building three blocks ahead of us. What do you mean we should give him one?"

"Where do you park?" Cars filled the limited spaces along the street.

"I do not need to see my OB, Xavier. The baby's fine."

"But we won't be if we don't get this guy off our tail. There has to be more parking than what's available on the street."

"There's a parking garage beneath the office building and a public garage a few blocks over."

"Beneath the building?" he questioned.

"You have to drive around to the other side of the building. What are you thinking?"

"I want to talk to this guy."

"Are you crazy?"

"Very possibly."

The half-formed idea was taking shape in his head. There wasn't time for detailed planning, but he thought he could make it work.

"I'm going to pull up in front of the office building. You jump out and run inside. He won't be expecting it and once you're in there he won't know where you've gone."

"He'll go after you!"

Xavier smiled without humor. "Exactly."

"We are not splitting up."

Traffic came to another stop. The green sedan was seven cars back. His half-formed idea was risky, but the two of them couldn't drive around forever and it was pointless to think he could outrun the other car or lose the guy without a miracle or a lot of luck.

"Zoe, I don't have time to argue with you. When I stop, jump out and run for the lobby."

"And you'll do what?"

She was frightened for him. He covered her cold hand with his. "I'm going to lead him around to the parking garage."

"Where he'll kill you," she told him flatly. "I appreciate your macho self-confidence. However, you'll recall you aren't armed and he is. In movies, the guy with the gun always wins."

The traffic light changed and the line of cars surged forward. He pulled his attention back to the busy street.

"I thought it was the hero who always won," he corrected lightly.

"The hero usually has a gun."

His lips quirked. "I'll have to take his then."

"That isn't funny."

"Zoe, I have the Taser and the pepper spray I took from the guard last night."

"Against a guy with a gun!"

His instructors would have said that was more than he needed, and he smiled. "I didn't say it was going to be easy."

"You'll get killed. You aren't even a real bodyguard. You run a charter boat!"

"I didn't always run a charter boat." He caught her troubled gaze. "Trust me. I'm not suicidal."

"That remains to be seen."

"The tall building on the corner up there, right?" Windows gleamed in the sun. The fifteen-story building filled the street corner.

"Yes."

The sidewalks bustled with people. If he screwed up, at least she'd be able to get away.

"You ready to do this?" he asked.

"No."

"Your part's easy. You go into the lobby and wait."

"This is stupid! I'm sorry your brother is dead, but I wish I'd never met him. And you're going to do this no matter what I say, aren't you?"

"Yes. Get ready."

"Do not get killed. I don't want to explain to my baby that his father and his uncle died trying to save my life."

His breath caught. "Uncle? Are you saying you're pregnant with *Wayne's* baby? Does Trent know?"

Her tone turned frosty. "Of course he knows." She tightened her grip on her purse. "Are we going to do this?"

Xavier stopped hard in front of the main entrance without warning. Brakes squealed behind them. They weren't rear-ended, but horns honked in exasperation as Zoe leaped from the car and ran for the front door, clutching her purse.

Xavier watched the man in the green sedan. Caught by surprise, he made no move to bring up a weapon. The minute Zoe was inside, Xavier continued through the traffic light and turned the corner.

There was no parking on the side street. Traffic was light there, so he sped up and whipped around to the back of the building. The parking garage was exactly where she'd said it would be.

Two other drivers pulled in behind him as Xavier turned in, took a ticket and drove deep inside the busy garage before finding a place to park. The other two cars had bought him enough time to get out of his car unseen before the green sedan cleared the entrance.

Keeping low, he darted around to the other side of a gray minivan parked beside his rental car. The elevator entrance was several yards away at his back. He didn't spare it a glance. The green sedan glided to a stop behind his rental car seconds later.

Crouched beside the rear wheel of the minivan, Xavier

waited, calling on his military training to find the zone. He was going to get only one shot at this.

ZOE URGED THE ELEVATOR to descend faster. If Xavier got killed, she would never forgive herself for going along with his stupid plan. The idea had been insane. A Taser and pepper spray against a gun. What had he been thinking?

Wayne's partners had already shown they were ready to kill everyone who got in their way. They knew Xavier had also seen their faces now. He was a bigger liability than she was. Yet he'd seemed so calm. So confident.

The idiot!

Stepping from the elevator hard on the heels of the other four people who rode down with her, Zoe hesitated at the opening of the garage to survey the dim interior. Xavier was nowhere in sight.

A green sedan had pulled up a few yards away, blocking several cars in place. The sedan's engine was running. The driver's door hung open. Where was the driver?

Her heart thudded painfully against her rib cage. She couldn't decide what to do. The concrete echoed with the sound of footsteps as people moved purposefully about the garage, intent on their own business. Other than an annoyed glance or two, no one paid any attention to the car that forced incoming and outgoing traffic to squeeze past.

As she crept closer, ready to dart down between cars, Zoe heard the unmistakable sound of a scuffle and flesh striking flesh. A head suddenly popped up between cars. A ginger-haired stranger hauled Xavier to his feet. Adrenaline flooded her system. There was a glint of metal in the man's hand.

Both men were breathing hard, their faces bright cherry-red. Tears coursed down their cheeks. But the wave of menace coming off Xavier was scary. He spun in a move almost too fast to follow, striking the man's arm. The gun bounced off the rental car and clattered to the concrete.

Zoe ran forward. A whiff of pepper spray nearly stopped her, but the gun was lying partially under the car parked next to Xavier's. Trying to stay clear of their silent struggle, Zoe bent to retrieve it. Someone bumped her hip. The ginger-haired man went sprawling to the pavement beside her.

"Zoe! Get out of here!"

Xavier moved past her, grabbing for the man. Her fingers closed over the barrel. The cold metal was surprisingly heavy in her hand.

Zoe moved back and pointed it at the stranger. "Hold it! I've got a gun!"

For a second they both froze. The stranger's expression was an odd mix of pain and relief. "Ms. Linden? Are you all right?"

"Give me the gun, Zoe," Xavier demanded at the same time.

Zoe shivered. "You can't even see!"

He scowled fiercely, blinking hard while he continued to grip the stranger firmly, but the fight seemed to have gone out of both men.

"There's bottled water on the floor in the backseat," Xavier growled at her.

"Then get it and wash your eyes out," she snapped. "Something's not right here."

The stranger, blinking rapidly, seemed to relax. "You're with this man willingly, Ms. Linden?"

"Zoe—"

She ignored Xavier, which was not easy to do when he looked so fierce. "Yes, I am. Who are you?"

"Eric Holmes. I work for Mark Ramsey of Ramsey Inc. Harrison Trent hired us to provide you with a bodyguard."

"I met my bodyguard, and you aren't him."

He inclined his head. "You met James Wickliff. I was his night relief man."

"Zoe—"

"He's right, Xavier. James Wickliff is the name of the man I met."

Xavier squinted at her. For a moment she thought he'd reach out and take the gun from her. Instead he released the other man and opened the back door of his car to fish out a bottle of water. After a second's hesitation, he grabbed a second one and handed it to the man he'd just been fighting with.

"Thanks."

She lowered the gun and waited while they poured water in their streaming eyes.

"I got to your place early the other night so James could introduce me to you," Eric Holmes told them as he flushed his eyes. "Damn, but this burns! I found James unconscious in the stairwell off the lobby. I was calling for help when I saw the two of you running through the parking lot."

"You can prove this?" Xavier demanded. He ignored the water running down his face and soaking his shirt.

"My P.I. license is in my wallet in my hip pocket. And just so you know, we're drawing a crowd."

He was right. Several people had stopped to stare at the scene. One woman was running to her car, holding her young son protectively.

"Uh, Xavier, he isn't kidding."

Xavier didn't take his eyes from the man. The Taser appeared in his hand. "Pull the wallet out. Slowly."

"No problem. I saw what your Taser did to James. Getting pepper-sprayed was enough."

"Not my Taser," Xavier corrected as the man slowly withdrew his wallet and held it out.

"Is Mr. Wickliff okay?" Zoe asked.

"I don't know, ma'am. They took James away in an ambulance."

Zoe inhaled and immediately coughed. The pepper spray still lingered and it was strong. Xavier passed her the wallet. She flipped it open. "The driver's license says Eric Ralph Holmes. It has his photo. The private investigator's license is the same."

"Mark Ramsey has everyone out looking for you, Ms. Linden. No offense, but we thought you were kidnapped."

"I nearly was," she admitted. "If it hadn't been for Xavier—"

"Let's move this show before the cops arrive," Xavier ordered, cutting her off. "Someone's bound to have used their cell phone to call them by now. Zoe, you drive. We'll take his car."

Without waiting, Xavier grabbed the shopping bag from the backseat and thrust it at Holmes. "You sit in the back, but keep your hands where I can see them at all times. Otherwise we'll find out if this Taser is as strong as the one they used on your buddy."

Eric Holmes grimaced, but obeyed the steel in Xavier's voice. Zoe wanted to protest that the man was on their side, but this didn't seem the time to argue, given the small crowd of onlookers. Xavier reached out and took the gun from her while Eric Holmes climbed into the backseat of his own car. Xavier pressed the Taser into her hand in exchange.

"What am I supposed to do with this?"

"Stick it in your waistband where you can get to it in a hurry." He reached back inside the car for the package of water.

Zoe was pretty sure arguing with Xavier in this mood was futile. Evidently, Holmes agreed. She slid behind the wheel of the unfamiliar car and adjusted the seat so she could reach the pedals comfortably while Xavier came around the car and opened the passenger door. He had to toss several paper cups and wrappers over the seat before he could even get inside but once he did, he turned so he could face Eric Holmes.

"Do not make a scene at the ticket booth," Xavier warned the other man.

"Hey, you're the one holding the gun."

Zoe smiled weakly. "Told you so. The guy with the gun always wins."

"Who are you?" Holmes demanded of Xavier as Zoe turned the car around and headed for the exit.

"Her new bodyguard."

"And you don't carry a gun?"

Her smile became a grin. Xavier didn't respond.

Zoe paid the man in the booth with the ten Xavier handed her. As she pulled onto the street she glanced at him. "Is now a good time to mention this could be construed as kidnapping and grand theft auto?"

"No. Where's the nearest car rental place?"

"I have no idea."

"The car has a GPS system," Holmes told them from the backseat.

"I noticed," Zoe agreed. "And at least a week's worth of old coffee cups and food wrappers."

In the rearview mirror she watched him shrug. "My cleaning lady's ill." Despite his red eyes he managed a wink.

"I like him," she told Xavier.

"Don't get too attached, we're going to dump him."

"Ouch," Eric Holmes protested.

"I thought the purpose of trapping him was to ask him some questions," Zoe objected.

"He's not one of the kidnappers."

Holmes leaned forward intently. "Who's been kidnapped?"

"Sit back," Xavier ordered. To Zoe he added, "Your former

bodyguard's night replacement isn't going to have answers to any of the questions we need to ask."

"Try me," their passenger suggested.

Xavier ignored his burning eyes to study the man. "Special Forces?"

Holmes eyed him with surprise and speculation. "Seventy-fifth Ranger Regiment a long time and thirty pounds ago. You?"

"Navy Seal. I work out a couple of times a week with a friend who was a Ranger. I thought I recognized a couple of those moves."

"Male bonding. How nice."

Xavier glanced at Zoe. She gave him a sugary smile. "Mind telling me where I'm going before you two start with the secret handshakes?"

"Head toward Arlington."

"Why Arlington?"

Because it would take them away from the church, but he wasn't going to say that out loud. "I'll explain later. What do you know about Wayne Drake?" Xavier asked Holmes.

"He was a thief and con man who liked wealthy people's money and expensive belongings, especially antique jewelry. He generally went after women, no offense, Ms. Linden, and charmed his way into their…" he hesitated "…lives."

Xavier didn't look at Zoe. The man wasn't saying anything they couldn't have learned from reading Wayne's police report, but he inclined his head at Holmes to continue.

"Drake generally worked alone although the police believe he's used a partner from time to time in the past. Their first assumption was that he was killed because of his association with Ms. Linden, but now they are wondering if the attempts on her life have been because of her association with him."

"What attempts?" Xavier demanded.

"I wasn't even seeing him anymore," Zoe protested.

Eric Holmes looked from one to the other. "Okay, are you two even talking to each other?"

Xavier scowled. "Apparently not."

"Hey," she protested. "When has there been time for conversation?"

"How long has someone been trying to kill you?" Xavier demanded.

"Three months or so. Right after I broke up with your brother someone took a shot at me as I came out of work one night. Harrison, Artie and I had just left the office. We parted in front of the doors and I was crossing the parking lot when someone in a car opened fire."

"So my brother's murder—"

She tensed. "Was probably my fault. Yes. If he hadn't been with me that night he might still be alive."

"Not necessarily," Holmes corrected. "The police believe it was your association with Mr. Drake that put you at risk."

"But the first incident happened *after* I stopped dating him."

He shrugged. "It's possible his killer didn't know that. And frankly, Mr. Drake was a thief. There's nothing in your background that shows a motive for someone to want you dead. It seems more likely that the attempt on your life was a strike at him. There were no further tries once you announced your engagement to Mr. Trent."

Xavier found his heart pounding.

"Until he was killed."

"*He* was killed. You weren't. Drake may have had a disgruntled partner or an ex-girlfriend."

Or an ex-wife who still loved him. Xavier hated the thought, but was it possible?

"And we know he had an ex-wife. The police have been looking into all those scenarios."

No wonder Sandy had refused to involve the police even

when her daughter had been kidnapped. Sandy loved her daughter, but the cops had probably been giving her a hard time. Her grief and despair over April were real and the men claimed they wanted a briefcase. That was consistent with the fact that Zoe had said both her place and Wayne's apartment had been trashed. Wayne must have double-crossed someone.

"Do the police know what Wayne was involved in recently?" Xavier asked.

"I don't think so, but if they do, they aren't saying."

Xavier hadn't expected any different. His brother had been smart and he'd known how to keep things to himself.

"Who are you working for?" Holmes asked Xavier.

"Me," Zoe responded.

"Uh-huh. But I know most of the professionals in this area and I don't know him."

Xavier held Holmes's gaze. "I'm not from this area."

They stared at each other. "I don't suppose you'd show me your credentials?"

"I don't suppose I would."

Zoe's grip on the steering wheel tightened. Xavier was surprised when she remained silent. Finally, Holmes inclined his head.

"You trust this man, Ms. Linden?"

Xavier waited.

"Yes."

He began to breathe again.

"Okay. This information stays here in this car. Our people do a lot of insurance work, so after Mr. Trent hired us, Mark went over the list of reported crimes dating back to before the first attempt on your life. Given Mr. Drake's past history, we were looking for a theft in his style, but big enough to have required a partner. One or two situations looked possible, but none required a partner. And none were significant enough to have provoked an attempted murder on you, Ms. Linden."

Xavier set his jaw. "People have killed for pocket change."

"But generally not professionals."

Zoe frowned. Her gaze remained on the crowded street in front of her and she didn't respond.

"Ms. Linden's condo and Drake's apartment were turned inside out a few days after his murder. That leads everyone to conclude that he pulled some sort of heist and that there was a partner, or someone who knew he had something of value."

Xavier could have added Sandy's home to that list, but he was the only one who knew about that since she had refused to tell the police anything. Her reticence made sense if the police had been questioning her about the attempts on Zoe.

That also made her anger with Zoe more reasonable. Not only had Wayne been dating Zoe while still married to Sandy, but Sandy probably saw Zoe as the reason Wayne was murdered. Maybe she was. It was starting to look as if a number of things were going on here.

"If someone is looking for something," Holmes continued, "why would they think you had it, Ms. Linden? No offense, but even if the two of you were sharing a residence—"

"We weren't."

"Then why rip your place apart? As I understand it, you and Drake had only seen each other for a couple of weeks before you broke up. You hadn't seen him for more than three months at the time of his death, right?"

She tapped the steering wheel absently. "That's true. That's why none of this makes any sense to me. The first attempt on my life happened after I stopped dating Wayne."

"Get to the point, Holmes," Xavier commanded.

"Okay. We know Drake was especially fond of glitter. His only arrest and conviction came because he had fenced a collection of antique jewelry they were able to trace back to one of his…married conquests. Now the only crime that even comes close to fitting the criteria we're looking for isn't his style, but it's the best lead we have. Three months ago, two people approached a bonded courier with a briefcase containing gemstones and gold outside his car. It was broad daylight."

Zoe tensed.

"The courier was shot and killed on the spot. While no one saw it happen, someone did see a couple of people walking away from the area with a briefcase. All the person noticed was that they were dressed in business attire."

"Wayne didn't like guns," Xavier stated flatly.

Holmes nodded. "I told you it didn't fit his MO, but gems do. As for the gun, obviously someone connected to him likes them."

For a moment no one spoke.

Xavier tried to picture his brother killing a man in cold blood and couldn't. "Wayne believed armed robbery was for brainless thugs. He liked what he called 'the game,' pitting himself against another person to achieve his goal. He never took from anyone who couldn't afford the loss and he never carried a weapon."

Holmes leaned forward. "Sounds like you knew Drake pretty well."

"I remember hearing about that robbery when it happened." Zoe's voice was thoughtful, saving Xavier from answering. "Didn't the police think it was an inside job? I don't recall any follow-up stories."

"They do, and there weren't many follow-up stories," Holmes agreed. "But the insurance company and the police are still working the case."

"Are you?" she asked.

"Officially? No, ma'am."

Xavier met her worried gaze. He shook his head, willing

her to silence. After a moment, the bodyguard sat back, again without taking his gaze from Xavier.

"If Drake was invited to participate in the heist without knowing his partner planned a murder, is it possible he took the briefcase and walked away?"

"I don't know," Xavier admitted. He hadn't spoken to his brother in years, but he thought a briefcase filled with gems might have been quite a draw. Except he didn't believe Wayne would condone cold-blooded murder.

Still, Xavier knew Zoe was thinking the same thing he was. As a motive, this scenario fit, right down to the missing briefcase—and the large rock Wayne had given to Zoe.

"You can see how it fits together," Holmes added as if listening to his thoughts. He studied them closely. "Drake's partner kills the courier. The two of them have a falling out over the murder. Drake takes the briefcase and his partner comes after him. Maybe he tries to kill Ms. Linden as a warning to Drake. 'Give me the case or else.' Ms. Linden and Drake suddenly split. The attempts on her life stop."

"And don't start up again until I have dinner with him once more months later? That doesn't sound like a partner to me," Zoe protested.

"It does if you consider that you weren't even hit in the shots that were fired the night Drake was killed. The shooter didn't care about you. He killed Drake, then went looking for the case."

"Then why come after me now?"

"The police think the killer believes you saw his face that night."

"I didn't."

Holmes shook his head. "It doesn't matter if you did or not. It's what the killer believes. Now that he has the case, he wants to tidy up."

"But he didn't—"

"Zoe!"

Holmes sat back with a look of satisfaction. "Didn't what, Ms. Linden? Find the case? How would you know that?"

"She doesn't have the briefcase." Xavier held his gaze. "Neither do I."

Holmes scratched his cheek. "But you do know something."

"I know a lot of things and none of them change anything."

"How's that?"

Xavier rubbed his jaw, feeling tired once again. "Wayne's partners are still coming after Zoe."

"Partners, plural?"

"There were two men at her place Friday night."

Zoe gave him a startled glance. "You said three."

"I was counting Holmes here as one of them. I saw you get out of your car in the parking lot and check your gun. That's why I rushed her out of the place. I thought *you* were Wayne's partner."

Holmes looked rueful. "It was a botch all the way around. Like we told Mr. Trent, if we're right that her boyfriend's partner is determined to kill her—"

"*Ex*-boyfriend," she corrected.

"Pardon me, ex-boyfriend. A bodyguard isn't going to be a deterrent. The safest thing she could do is leave the country like she was supposed to do this afternoon."

"We had honeymoon tickets to Italy," Zoe informed Xavier.

"And what was going to happen when you got back?" Xavier asked.

"We were hoping the police would have them in custody by then."

"So who was kidnapped?" Holmes asked.

"Time to drop you somewhere," Xavier told him.

"I could help."

"I don't think so." The fewer people who knew about

April's kidnapping the better. "Except that we'll need to borrow your car for a little bit."

"And the gun," Zoe added, with a meaningful glance at Xavier. "Where would you like us to drop you, Mr. Holmes?"

"I suppose the nearest police station is out of the question."

She smiled at him in the rearview mirror. "I'm sorry. Really. I don't guess we could ask you not to report this?"

Holmes regarded them steadily. "I'm going to reach in my pocket for a business card," he told Xavier. "It has my cell-phone number. When you're done, call me and tell me where you leave my car, okay? I can't afford to replace it right now."

Xavier studied his face. Like Zoe, he felt a grudging respect for the bodyguard who was now sporting a bruise on one cheek to go with his blotchy face and red eyes. "Why?"

"Let's just call it professional courtesy, one bodyguard to another. I don't want to see anything bad happen to this lady."

Curtly, Xavier nodded. "Neither do I."

Chapter Seven

They dropped Eric Holmes off near a hotel where he could easily get a cab or call someone to pick him up.

"Do you think he'll call the police?" Zoe asked.

"No, I don't think he will." Holmes's parting words had been *Try not to shoot anyone with my gun.*

"So now what? Do we ask the machine here how to find a car rental place?"

Xavier debated. He didn't believe Holmes would call the police, but he'd bet all he owned the man called his boss before they were even out of sight. Renting another car would eat up valuable time they didn't have.

"Hey, you awake over there, Xavier? While you're thinking, I need to find a bathroom. And could we eat something? I'm starving."

She had to be kidding. "You just ate a steak and eggs smothered in peanut butter."

"That was over an hour ago."

"Are you serious?"

"Of course I am. Time really does fly when you're having fun. All the excitement made me hungry." Zoe slanted him a quick glance as she coasted to a stop at the next traffic light. "You can be pretty intimidating when you work at it, you know."

He scowled. "You wouldn't have seen me being intimidating if you had waited for me in the lobby like you should have. What were you thinking, coming down to the parking garage that way?"

She narrowed her eyes. "That maybe even a scary, intimidating man like you might need some help."

Fear for her lent terseness to his words. "You could have been seriously hurt, Zoe. If you don't want to think about yourself, think of the baby. You can't be taking risks like that."

Zoe took a deep breath and then another. It didn't help. She had sat in on more than one hostile meeting over the years. She could certainly deal with Xavier, as well.

"I will try to accept that this macho aggression comes from genuine concern and not gender bias—'me big strong man, you helpless little woman'—"

"I didn't say—"

"—but I wish to remind you that I am sitting here with a Taser that *you* gave me. And being a *not* so helpless little woman, you should know that my control isn't exactly what it should be at the moment, so I suggest we move on."

His surprised expression would have been comical under other circumstances. Satisfied she'd made her point, Zoe continued wryly. "Now, I promise not to let anyone else drop me off a balcony—which is obviously where I went wrong with you in the first place—if we can shelve this conversation and find a bathroom and a place to eat. I wonder if any of the fast-food places make a peanut butter milkshake."

His silence was a tad scary. Abruptly, his shoulders relaxed and his lips curved at the corners. "So pregnant women really do crave pickles and ice cream?"

She allowed a disdainful sniff. "Peanut butter and ice cream is much more satisfying."

ZOE SIPPED AT THE plain vanilla milkshake she'd purchased at a fast-food drive-through while Xavier ran into a nearby store to purchase a cell-phone charger so he could call his former sister-in-law. Meeting Sandy for the first time was bound to be uncomfortable, but April was all that was important here. Just thinking of the little girl in the hands of cold-blooded killers made Zoe feel ill.

That Xavier loved his niece was obvious every time he mentioned her. Zoe could see his grief and his impatience to find her. He was willing to go to any extreme to rescue the child, and she desperately wanted to help him.

Zoe touched her rounded stomach. Xavier would be her child's uncle as well. She suspected that was why he'd been so upset with her earlier. Xavier was the sort of man who protected those he cared about, and he'd basically told Eric Holmes that that protection extended to her.

Her stomach fluttered at the thought. She set aside the milkshake to dig through her purse for her cell phone. Artie had told her that he'd called several times, but she'd never heard the cell phone ring. Surely Harrison would try to call her now that he wasn't someone's captive. Or was he? Who was the beautiful woman he'd been with? And wasn't it telling that she didn't feel anything more than concern for his welfare?

Zoe pulled out the phone. It was set to vibrate instead of ring, and she had missed seven calls. Two were from Artie, one was from the wedding planner, and one was a number she didn't recognize. The rest were from her friends and members of the wedding party. All had left messages, but it was the unrecognizable number that caused hope to bloom.

"Ms. Linden, this is Detective Marcus Frowleigh with the Alexandria Police Department. Please give me a call…"

Zoe disconnected as Xavier slid into the car.

"Problem?"

"The police department wants me to call." A shiver went down her spine.

"What did you tell them?"

"It was a voice message."

"How long ago?"

"Eight-twelve."

Xavier relaxed. "Trent didn't call?"

"No." Her concern deepened. Why hadn't he called? He'd gone to the church. He must have spoken to Artie by now. He'd know she hadn't stood him up.

"I'm sorry, Zoe." He sounded guilty. Why? "He's probably tied up with the police."

She brightened. "I hadn't thought of that. You got a charger?"

"One for each of us."

Xavier handed her the one for her phone and plugged his into the car receptacle. The moment he started the engine his phone began to ring. He didn't look at the display. "That will be April's mother."

Zoe nodded.

"Hello."

"Xavier, where have you been?"

Zoe winced as Sandy's frantic voice carried to her.

"What's happened? Is it April?" Xavier's tone became sharp.

"I tried to call you all night!"

"My cell phone needed recharging, Sandy. What's wrong?"

"They called. The kidnappers want to meet. They want to exchange Wayne's little friend for April."

XAVIER DIDN'T LOOK at Zoe as his jaw tightened.

"They said they'd kill her, Xavier! They said they're tired of playing games. They want the woman. I know you believe she isn't involved, but April's life is at stake! You have to meet them. You have to give them that tramp Wayne was sleeping with! I want my daughter back."

And she began to cry. His heart constricted. His brother had so much to answer for.

"Did they say anything about Trent?" he asked her.

"Who?"

"Harrison Trent. Zoe's fiancé."

"Why would they care about him? All they want is the briefcase."

So Sandy didn't know what had gone down at the Van Wheeler estate. She wasn't the most stable personality at the best of times, but she loved her daughter and if she knew Wayne's partners had gone after Zoe's fiancé, she'd be totally hysterical.

"All right, Sandy. When and where do they want to meet?"

"They said they'd call me back at one. You'll do it? You'll trade the woman for April?"

Zoe's expression was stricken. He knew she could hear every word. "I told you I'd get your daughter back and I will." He held Zoe's gaze. "You have to trust me."

"I do. But you said we couldn't trade one life for another. You said—"

He continued to hold Zoe's gaze. "Trust me. Will you do that?"

Zoe inclined her head. Xavier looked away as Sandy let out a long breath.

"Schedule a meet with them and call me back."

Sandy sniffed. "All right."

"Call me the minute you hear from them."

"Yes. I will. Where are you?"

"Taking care of a few things. Don't worry, Sandy. I'll bring April home."

"I don't know what I'd do without you, Xavier."

"Hang in there. It will be over soon. Call me when you hear from them. It's going to be all right. I promise." He prayed that he wasn't lying, and then he disconnected.

"You heard all that?" he asked Zoe.

"Yes." She reached out and covered his hand. "I'll help you get her back, Xavier."

He nodded, the compassion in her face making him too emotional to respond for a moment. Every time he let himself think about what might be happening to his niece, he wanted to hit something. He understood how Sandy felt. He hated feeling helpless.

"What's the plan?" Zoe asked.

"I don't have one." He regarded her bleakly. "But I'm not going to trade one life for another."

"Of course not. But I don't mind being bait."

"I mind," he told her fiercely, surprised by how strongly he meant those words. He would not allow this woman to be placed in danger, not even to save April.

Her eyes warmed. "We have a gun."

"So do they and there are two of them that we know of."

"Ah, yes, but they aren't you. The hero with the gun always wins."

He didn't return her smile. "This isn't a movie, Zoe, and I'm no hero."

"It may not be a movie, but I'm betting on my bodyguard. Those two don't have a chance."

He wanted to kiss her. She was gazing at him with such naked trust he wanted to pull her into his arms and taste those soft lips.

"You missed your wedding," he reminded her gruffly instead.

"Yes."

Just that. Her tone had flattened. Xavier would have given much to know what she was thinking right then. "Shouldn't you be more upset?"

"Probably."

"What does that mean?"

"I realized this morning that Harrison and I were getting married for the wrong reason."

He followed the motion as her hand went to her stomach. "I thought you said it was Wayne's baby."

She blinked and raised her chin defiantly. "It is, but Harrison didn't care. He knew how much I wanted to give my child the sort of loving family I grew up with."

Xavier waited, watching her features for clues to what she was thinking.

"I lost my parents and my brother in a plane crash when I was in college. My dad was a good pilot, but an engine malfunctioned. The plane hit a power line when he tried to bring it down. They were still a mile out from the airport. He managed to miss a subdivision, but there were no survivors on the plane."

Her grief was obvious. "I'm sorry."

Zoe nodded and drew a deep breath. "Survivor guilt is hard to live with at times. We were a close-knit family. I want that for my child. But—" she looked away and then turned back, shaking her head "—I rushed into this without thinking things through."

"What does that mean?"

"Our marriage would have been a mistake."

Because of him? He tried to sort through the confusing surge of emotions. People were known to fall in love with their rescuers, but that wasn't real, either. Xavier didn't want to be her third mistake. "Left it a bit late for that decision, didn't you?"

Zoe surprised him again with a wistful smile. "Almost too late. I think we should grab some lunch before April's mother calls back, don't you?"

He recognized a change of subject when he heard one. "You just had a milkshake."

"Only a little of it and I'm eating for two. There's room for lunch."

"You sure you aren't having triplets?"

Her laugh was weak and he realized she was nervous. She'd just revealed a part of herself to him and was probably regretting the fact. Impulsively, he reached out and squeezed her hand. "I won't let them hurt you, Zoe."

"I know you won't."

The trust in her gaze hit him where he lived. Xavier gave over to the impulse that had been urging him on since last night. He leaned across the seat and cupped her face in his hands. Her eyes widened. She drew in a breath. He gave her time to pull away, holding her gaze. The pulse in her throat jumped rapidly, but she didn't pull back. So he touched the spot lightly with the tip of his tongue. She sucked in another breath and he captured her lips.

He had intended it to be a simple kiss, but the moment their lips met it turned into something quite different. Liquid fire raced through his veins. Her hands wound around his neck as she kissed him back, pulling him closer. With a groan, he turned it into a searching kiss, sampling her and feeling drunk on the sensations.

Abruptly, she pulled free. He let her go and sat back. There was dismay and guilt in her stunned expression.

"Should I apologize?" he managed gruffly.

Her fingers shook. She brushed a strand of hair away from her face and shook her head. "No."

But she wouldn't meet his eyes.

"Let's find a restaurant."

HIS KISS HAD SHAKEN Zoe completely. Nothing had ever felt so right—or been so wrong. She welcomed the crowded restaurant with its noisy families and groups of shoppers. She ordered a steak-topped salad and sat toying with a roll while they waited.

"Don't."

"What?" Zoe met his eyes for the first time since he'd kissed her.

"Stop torturing the roll. We're in an impossible situation here, Zoe. It would be strange if we weren't attracted to one another. It was only a kiss. Don't worry about it."

"Only a kiss?" She set aside the mangled roll. "Like Mount Saint Helens was only a volcano?"

"Okay, poor choice of words."

"Darn right." Heat bloomed in her cheeks. She could still feel the tingle of his lips on hers as though she were some teenager who'd been kissed for the first time. Hadn't she already told herself no tingles? "But don't worry, I'm not about to read anything into a minor kiss. Tell me about April."

The waitress arrived with their food before he could say anything. Xavier's now troubled expression made her feel a little better, however.

"I didn't say it was a minor kiss," he told her as soon the woman left.

"Good, because I think the less you say right now the better."

He sat back and watched her through narrowed eyes. "I haven't felt like a bungling teenager since—"

"Please spare me the details of your sex life. As you said, it was only a kiss."

"A mind-blowing—"

Zoe shook her head as her cheeks heated some more. "Tell me about April."

With a look she couldn't fathom, he finally stopped staring at her and picked up his fork. "All right, but this discussion is merely tabled for now. April is a great kid," he told her and his entire demeanor changed. His features softened and worry returned to underscore his words.

"She's a bright, quiet, undemanding little girl. And she

loves working on the boats with her cousins when she comes to visit. My family's a loud, rambunctious group. They can be pretty overwhelming at first, but once she gets used to the commotion again she fits right in. My sister Lorraine has a daughter her age, and Darlene has a girl a couple of years older. The three of them are fast friends."

Love filled his voice. As he talked about his family and the life they'd built together in Florida, she saw him in a different way from the hard, cold, efficient bodyguard she had come to know. His family sounded a lot like hers had been, only on a larger scale.

"Sounds like there are a lot of you."

Xavier nodded. "Three sisters, three in-laws and the families that go with them, nine nieces and nephews and my mom and dad."

"Where do you fit into that lineup?" she asked, as she picked the meat from her salad.

"Lorraine and Darlene are older than me and Audra is younger. Wayne was the baby."

His brother's name hung in the air between them like some uninvited ghost. Zoe set down her fork.

"Something wrong with the salad?" he asked.

The warm concern in his voice made her reach for her water glass to cover the emotions threatening to swamp her. Hearing about his family had made her miss her own more than usual. And Wayne's name reminded her of the mess she'd made of her current situation. "I guess I had too much milkshake after all."

He set aside his plate as well, his sandwich and fries barely tasted. "I'll get the check."

They left the restaurant in oddly companionable silence. Zoe was fully aware of him at her side, but it felt nice. Xavier was a restful companion when he chose to be. Definitely not high energy like his brother had been.

His cell phone rang as he started the car. His former sister-in-law's voice was shrill with suppressed excitement and once again carried to where Zoe sat.

"They called, Xavier! They want you to meet at 2:30 p.m. at the Kirchner Business Park in Arlington. Do you know where that is?"

Zoe frowned and gestured toward the GPS system.

"No," he told her flatly. "Call them back. Tell them I'll meet them at Stanton Lake. The place where I take April when I'm in town."

"Call them back? How can I call them back?" she shrilled.

Xavier's voice remained calm, but firm. "You've got caller ID, Sandy. Did they block the number?"

"No, but it was just a phone number."

Zoe raised her eyebrows. Technology challenged, or just stupid?

Xavier shook his head. "Read me the number. I'll call them back."

"Xavier, you can't! They might kill her."

"Read me the number, Sandy."

Even Zoe wouldn't have argued with that tone. Sandy sputtered another second before haltingly calling out the number. Zoe found herself breathing hard. While a business park seemed a strange choice for an exchange, at least it would be empty on a hot, muggy Saturday afternoon. Not so a park, but it was obvious Xavier had some sort of plan.

"Xavier, are you sure about this? What if—"

"I'm not going to let anything happen to April, Sandy. It will be okay."

"But what if they refuse? What if they don't bring April?" she demanded. "What if it's a trick?"

Zoe was sure that was exactly what it was. After all, these men wanted her dead.

"They aren't going to try anything until they get the brief-case," Xavier told her, with a confidence Zoe was certain he didn't feel.

"I don't like this."

Neither did Zoe.

"I'll call you after I talk to them."

Zoe thought she could hear the other woman crying.

"Sandy. It's going to be okay. Stay by the phone."

He disconnected and regarded Zoe with bleak eyes. "Do you think they'll agree to change the meeting?" she asked.

"Only one way to find out." He hit the speaker button so Zoe could hear both sides of the conversation and punched in the number Sandy had given him.

"Hello?"

A man's deep, hoarse voice answered. Zoe was certain she'd never heard it before.

"This is Xavier Drake. I'm Wayne's brother."

"Son of a bitch. How'd you get—"

"You want the briefcase? I want my niece. And I have the woman, so I'm changing the plans. I'll meet you at Stanton Lake in Arlington. There's an old ice-cream shack near the dock. The place caught fire a few months ago. It's been boarded over, but you can't miss it. I'll bring the woman, you bring April and we'll trade."

There was a pause as if the man was trying to digest what he'd heard. "How do I know you'll do what you say?"

Xavier's bared teeth held no trace of humor. "Same way I know you'll keep your end of the bargain."

This time the pause was longer. "Maybe you already got the goods."

"I'm not in the same line as my brother." The ice in his voice chilled even Zoe. "The woman and the case are your problem. All I want is my niece."

There was another longish pause while it sounded as if the other man was saying something to someone out of phone range. Zoe couldn't hear him, only the murmur of his voice until he spoke once more.

"I don't trust you."

"We're even. How do I know you have April and she's still alive?"

The voice turned oily. Zoe imagined the other man sneering. "Guess you'll just have to take my word for it."

"Not good enough," Xavier told him firmly. "I want to talk to her."

"You think I'm stupid?"

"Only if you don't let me talk to her."

"This call's taking too long. You called the cops, didn't you? Ike, the damn bitch called the cops."

"No, she didn't." Xavier's voice remained calm and firm, but his knuckles were white with tension. "I'm April's uncle and she's far more valuable to me than whatever is in that case you want so badly."

"What about the woman?"

Xavier looked an apology at Zoe. "What about her?"

"How do I know she's got the case?"

"That's your problem."

"How do I know you've even got her? This sounds like a trap."

Xavier's eyes pleaded with her. It was almost as though Zoe could hear his thoughts, asking for her help. He extended the phone toward her.

Zoe opened her mouth and unplanned words simply tumbled out. "I'm not saying anything to anyone, you bastard."

Xavier thanked her with a look and the cold but reassuring hand he laid on her arm.

"Satisfied?" he asked the other man.

Again there was a pause that seemed to go on forever. Zoe

realized she was holding her breath. She released it slowly. Finally, a childish voice spoke.

"Uncle Xavier?"

"April! I'm coming for you, sweetheart."

"There," the man said before he'd finished speaking. "Now we both know where we stand. You bring the woman, I'll bring the kid. Four o'clock."

"Make it seven. I'm not walking a tied-up woman down to the shack in broad daylight."

"I got news for you, pal—it's still daylight at seven."

"Not tonight. The radio said it's supposed to rain. The park should be dark and deserted. Do we have a deal?"

Zoe could hear the speaker talking to someone else before he came back more clearly. "If I see one cop—"

"You won't."

"I better not, Drake, or there'll be another dead duck, this time floating in the water."

The connection broke. Xavier closed his eyes and didn't move for several seconds. His hand wasn't completely steady as he closed his cell phone. "Thank you."

Her throat was thick with too many emotions. "Tell me you have a plan."

"I'm working on it." He opened the phone and dialed another number. Sandy answered immediately.

"We're going to make the trade tonight at seven at the lake," he told her without preamble. "They have April. She spoke my name so I know she's alive."

"What about the woman?"

Zoe grimaced. Sandy made "the woman" sound like something she'd scraped off the bottom of her shoe.

"Let me worry about Zoe. I need to go now, Sandy. Don't worry yourself into a frenzy, all right? Let me handle this."

"As if I have a choice. You'll call me as soon as you have her?"

"I promise. You'll have her back tonight."

"Thank you, Xavier."

"Thank me when we have April. Hang tough." He disconnected and turned to Zoe. "Do you want to charge your cell phone? You can use mine to call Van Wheeler and see if Trent has checked in with him yet."

Her stomach tightened as she realized she hadn't given Harrison a thought. "Thank you." Zoe plugged her jack into the outlet and accepted Xavier's cell phone.

She hesitated before punching in Artie's number. "There's something I have to ask—was Wayne's wife still in love with him?"

He rubbed the back of his neck, looking weary. "Yes. I think so. And I know what you're thinking."

"Even I'm not sure what I'm thinking right now."

"You think Sandy might be the one who tried to kill you." She couldn't deny it. "And?"

Xavier sighed. "I'd like to say 'no way.'"

"But you can't?"

"Not and be totally honest with you. The truth is, that was the first thought that popped into my head, given the timing of the first attack. Sandy's an emotional person, but she isn't stupid. And I can guarantee you that she was the first person the police checked into. I suspect that's why she was so adamant I not call them in when April was taken. They gave her a bad time a few years ago when they tried to nail Wayne for another theft. I imagine this was worse. I'm sure they questioned her hard about Wayne's murder. Her only alibi was April."

Zoe felt a twinge of sympathy for the unknown woman.

"They may not have been divorced, but the process began long before Wayne met you, Zoe. This wasn't even the first time they'd separated. Like I said, Sandy isn't stupid. I know my brother and so did she. You wouldn't have been the first woman he pursued after he left Sandy."

"That makes me feel special."

"I'm being honest. Wayne liked women—the more, the better. Sandy knew it. She never wanted the divorce," he continued, "but she'd already held on to Wayne far longer than I would have said was possible."

"Because of April?"

"Most likely. My brother had few morals, but he loved his daughter. And if Sandy had gone after every woman my brother bedded, there'd be a string of dead women leading right to her front door."

"So you think Mr. Holmes was right? Wayne's partners shot at me as a warning to Wayne?"

"I don't know, but it's the most likely possibility."

Zoe shook her head. "As much as I hate to say it, why would they go after me and not his daughter? If he loved her so much, April would have been a better threat."

Xavier was shaking his head. "I think it's safe to say his partners knew nothing of April or Sandy when all this started. Wayne wasn't living with them and he would have kept them far away from everyone connected with his work. He never mentioned April to you, yet you say he proposed to you."

"He did propose."

"I don't doubt you. I'm just saying Wayne knew how to keep a secret when it suited him. I suspect one of his partners followed him and saw him with you. They seized on the chance and tried to spook him by making you a target."

"Seems like a stretch to me."

"Well, the other possibility is that the attempts on your life had nothing to do with Wayne or this situation."

"I don't know what to think. If Wayne's partners didn't know about April, how did they come to kidnap her?"

Xavier's frown deepened. "At a guess they learned about Sandy when she claimed his body from the morgue. I don't think they ever intended to kidnap April. We're pretty sure she walked in on them while they were trashing Sandy's house looking for the briefcase."

Zoe's cell phone chimed before she could respond. She snatched it up eagerly even though the number wasn't one she recognized.

"Hello?"

"Zoe?"

"Harrison? Harrison, where are you? Are you all right?"

Chapter Eight

Xavier tensed as Zoe spoke into the phone.

"I'm fine. Where are you? Are *you* okay? I saw you at the church…. Of course, I knew you'd go there if you could. What happened at Artie's house? How did you get away?"

Xavier wished he could hear the other side of her conversation, but Harrison's deep rumble didn't carry to where he sat, and Xavier needed to pay attention to the mechanical voice of the GPS system.

"He's in the hospital," Zoe continued. "Wayne's people showed up at the condo last night. We had to run and… In Arlington… No, Xavier's with me. We're… Carter Hughes? Why should I— Harrison? Harrison!"

"Zoe?" She faced Xavier with wide, frightened eyes. "What's going on?" he demanded.

"Harrison told me to call Carter Hughes and then the phone went dead."

"Cell phones drop in and out, you know that. It doesn't mean anything. He'll probably call back. What did he say?"

She practically vibrated with tension. "He wanted to speak to my bodyguard, but before I could explain about you he said there wasn't time and I should go to Carter Hughes."

Scowling, Xavier felt himself tensing. "Isn't that his lawyer?"

"Yes. Why would he tell me to go to him?"

Xavier had no idea, but he didn't like the way the man's name kept popping up.

"I'll call him," Zoe decided.

Pressing his hand over hers to stop her, Xavier shook his head. "Do it later. We need to get you someplace safe."

Her immediate reaction was to protest, but common sense kicked in as her stomach fluttered. "All right."

Xavier blinked in outright surprise.

"Thought I'd be chomping at the bit to go with you? I am, but these men want to kill me. I'm not going to make it easy for them."

"You always surprise me."

"Good. I hate to be predictable."

Xavier nearly smiled. The sun hit the tangled silk of her hair and she tossed back her head, tucking a strand behind her left ear. The image hit him viscerally. There was nothing provocative in the way she gazed at him, yet his breath caught all the same. He wanted her.

Those wide intelligent eyes missed little. She'd known exactly what to say when he'd thrust the phone at her and he had a feeling she was reading him just as easily right now. He wondered if his brother had appreciated how special she was.

He'd known and dated more beautiful women. The Florida beaches were a magnet for the flashy redheads, slinky blondes and even mysterious brunettes in their scraps of material that put everything on display. Yet none of them had ever held their heads tilted at just that angle with the sun brushing the tantalizing curve of her jaw. His gaze slid down the graceful line of her throat and he told himself not to be a fool.

"What?"

Her gaze was quizzical, but there was knowledge and

awareness in those intelligent eyes. She raised a graceful hand to brush nervously at another wisp of hair.

He was going to make a complete fool of himself. Xavier opened his mouth anyhow. "I think you're going to have to slap me."

"What for?"

"This." He leaned across the console, tilted her face up with a knuckle and captured the exquisite softness of her lips once again, moving down to nibble at her throat and touch the spot with his tongue when she shivered.

He was being ten kinds of fool and he didn't care. Her mouth was achingly sweet. And instead of pulling away like she should have done, she braced her hands on his shoulders.

He had no defense against the slow, sensual glide of her tongue across his lips. He could have taken her right then.

He opened his mouth. She accepted the invitation to deepen the kiss, consuming rational thought for a timeless moment. Fully aroused at her small sound of pleasure, Xavier forced himself to pull back. He sat for a moment with his forehead pressed to hers, breathing hard as he struggled for command of his body.

She lifted her flushed face. He was relieved to see her control was no better than his. Elation roared through him. She wanted him, too.

"What are we doing?" she asked softly.

"Looking to get arrested for lewd and indecent behavior."

"I think I like the sound of that."

With a strangled chuckle he reluctantly let her go. The tip of her tongue touched her lips as if seeking a last taste of him. He nearly groaned out loud, wanting nothing more than to finish what he'd started.

Color suffused her cheeks. Emotions flickered in the depths of her eyes. She lowered those thick, dark lashes to conceal them. He rubbed his thumb lightly over her swollen lips before starting the engine.

He couldn't believe he'd let a little sunshine on her hair distract him that way. April was out there somewhere, scared out of her mind and alone while he'd been making out with his dead brother's ex-girlfriend.

The thought of April jarred him back to reality more effectively than an ice-water bath. Xavier snapped closed all personal thoughts of Zoe. Focus on the mission. Locate April. Rescue her.

"While that was very nice, Xavier—very, very nice—and I appreciate your concern for my welfare, I can't let you go meet them alone." She held up her palm. "No, I don't mean me. It's time to bring in the police."

Scowling, because he knew she was right, he glanced in the rearview mirror. "Maybe I won't have to."

"What are you talking about? Oh."

A car pulled up behind theirs, trapping them in the parking space. Eric Holmes climbed out of the backseat. A man she'd never seen before stepped from behind the wheel. A third man left the passenger's seat and started in her direction.

"How?" she asked.

"GPS tracking system," Xavier answered calmly.

"They could be the police."

"Then it's a good thing you know that attorney."

"That isn't funny."

"I know. Put your palms flat on the dashboard and don't move until they tell you. I don't want to chance one of them is trigger-happy."

She hadn't seen any guns, but Zoe obeyed as Xavier splayed his hands over the steering wheel. "My life used to be so normal."

Dimples appeared as he smiled at her and Eric Holmes

rapped on his window. The man who had come up beside her tried to open the passenger door. She'd automatically locked it when she'd gotten inside and she saw no reason to open it now.

"It's okay. Open the door, Ms. Linden."

"Ms. Linden, are you all right?" Eric Holmes called out.

"Of course. We just had lunch."

Xavier's smile widened. He was relieved when she smiled back at him.

Eric Holmes looked amused as well. The man beside her, however, scowled darkly. "Get out of the car, Ms. Linden."

Xavier watched her hackles rise.

"I'm fine right here, thank you."

Xavier turned to Eric Holmes. "Guess you want your car back. I owe you a tank of gas."

"Ms. Linden—" the one at her window began again.

"Go away," she told him.

"It's okay, Terry," Holmes told the other man. "Would you both step out of the car, please? We don't want to draw another crowd."

"Might be a little late," Xavier warned, nodding toward a young couple who'd paused a few yards away to watch. "Might as well do what they say, Zoe." He shut off the ignition and reached for the door handle. Holmes stepped back to allow him out of the car.

With obvious reluctance, Zoe opened her door. But when the man called Terry would have reached to help her, she shook her head in warning. "I like to be introduced before I let someone touch me."

"That's Terry Prichard," Eric told her over the car hood as she stood up. A hint of laughter twinkled in his eyes and he winked at her. "And this is our boss, Mark Ramsey."

Xavier forced himself to appear relaxed. Zoe was taking her cues from him and he didn't want her to cause any trouble.

"You look like a cop." She scowled at Terry Prichard.

"Ex-cop," Eric told her cheerfully.

"Do we need the police, Ms. Linden?" the one called Mark Ramsey asked softly. Xavier knew he was the one to watch. Despite letting the other two speak first, he was the one in control here.

"That depends on whether Mr. Holmes plans to file grand theft auto charges," Xavier replied, holding his gaze.

"Not at the moment," Holmes responded. "Doesn't look like you got a ding on her."

"No, but there might be peanut butter cracker crumbs inside."

"Oh, that's funny." Zoe managed a glare for Xavier as she came around the back of the car, tailed closely by a solemn Terry Prichard.

"And you would be Xavier Drake?" Mark Ramsey asked.

He raised his eyebrows and inclined his head at Holmes. "You guys are fast. I'm pretty sure I didn't give Mr. Holmes my name."

"Ms. Linden?" Ramsey asked for confirmation.

Zoe shrugged. "I'm impressed, too. I told him there wasn't much of a family resemblance."

"Would you like to see my identification?" Xavier asked.

"If you don't mind."

Holmes stopped him as his hand started for his wallet.

"You aren't planning to reach for my gun, by any chance, are you?"

Xavier hadn't given the weapon a thought. "Nope. As a matter of fact, you're welcome to have it back. I don't have a permit, so if the cops do show up, I'd rather you were the one holding it." Xavier removed the gun slowly under the watchful eyes of all three men.

Eric checked the clip and nodded at his boss. "It hasn't been fired."

"Well, that did it," Zoe warned them. "I think that woman over there just called the police."

Ramsey glanced at the excited-looking woman speaking rapidly into her cell phone. He nodded at her in a business-like gesture and glanced down at Xavier's proffered wallet. "Okay. We'll take you home now, Ms. Linden."

Zoe's gaze flashed to Xavier before returning to Ramsey. "Which 'home' would that be, Mr. Ramsey?"

"Trent's place would be safest," Xavier pointed out. "There's better security there."

"We'll see that she's safe," Prichard growled.

"Does that mean you think you can do a better job now than you did the other night?"

Prichard glowered, but Ramsey didn't bristle. Eric Holmes flushed.

"Eric, Mr. Drake can ride with you and Terry. I'll take Ms. Linden in my car."

Zoe narrowed her eyes. "I'll stay with Xavier," she told him in a coldly officious tone that probably had people scurrying to obey when she was working. "No offense, Mr. Ramsey, but when it comes to bodyguards, I prefer Xavier."

"That right?" The dark-haired man gazed from one to the other. "Maybe I should be offering you a job, Mr. Drake."

Xavier couldn't stop the curve of his lips. Zoe had aligned herself firmly in his corner. "Thanks, but I already have one and so far, she's pretty much full-time."

Zoe stuck her tongue out at him. Holmes snorted a chuckle. Even Ramsey looked amused as he quickly reasserted control. "Very well, then. We need to finish this conversation some-place private. If the two of you would be so kind as to take the backseat of my car? Terry, you can ride shotgun and Eric can follow in his car."

"That's acceptable, but I'll be wanting my peanut butter crackers," Zoe told Holmes.

Prichard's frown deepened. "I thought you just ate."

"There is always room for peanut butter."

ERIC HOLMES HAD TO find a place to park on the street since Zoe didn't have a guest pass for the garage with her. He had to wait for clearance at the front desk while they entered through the underground garage. The garage didn't look any different in the daylight. The same cars appeared to be parked and the housekeeper's Porsche was still in its assigned slot, so there was no way to know if the mysterious Leon was inside or not.

Zoe called out as soon as they were inside, but no one answered. Nothing appeared to have been disturbed since they'd left the place the night before. Mark Ramsey waited until everyone was seated inside the luxury condo before the questions started.

"I'd offer you something to eat or drink, but there probably isn't much of either. We expected to be in Italy tonight," Zoe told the men matter-of-factly, "and Leon is missing. He was scheduled to fly home to visit his family tonight, but his mother's been quite ill." She looked at Xavier. "I didn't think about that the other night. If she took a turn for the worse he probably had to fly out early."

"Leon being?" Ramsey prompted.

Xavier smiled wryly. "The housekeeper. Ex–pro footballer, drives the green Porsche that was parked downstairs."

Ramsey didn't blink an eye. "I'll check it out," he promised. "You want to tell us what happened, Ms. Linden?"

"When?"

"Start with Friday night when I assume you met Mr. Drake."

Zoe looked to him for guidance. Xavier nodded for her to start.

"You want the long or the short version?"

"The short will be fine for now. If I have questions, I'll ask."

Zoe settled on the plush couch beside Xavier. "Xavier told me we had to leave because there were men downstairs with guns. We ran into them coming up the stairs, but he managed to get us out of the building and…" She looked to him once more.

"We drove to my motel room so she could change and try to reach her fiancé. She couldn't, so we left."

"When we did, someone tried to shoot us from a moving car," she added. "They wounded Xavier."

"A graze." He shrugged it off even though the wound still hurt. "But it was enough to tell me these men were playing hardball."

"How did you come to be involved, Mr. Drake?"

"My brother died in her arms. I wanted some answers. Only, when I got to her place, I saw I needed to keep her alive to get those answers."

"Just like that."

He met Ramsey's gaze with a tight one of his own. "Exactly like that."

"He's done a good job to date," Zoe put in quickly, obviously sensing the testosterone in the air. "We've been staying one jump ahead of them all day."

"So, you're what, Mr. Drake? Acting as a vigilante to discover who killed your brother?"

Ramsey wanted to provoke him, but Xavier didn't rise to the bait. He stretched out his legs and crossed them at the ankle. "Nope. Just looking for answers to what happened and why."

"Your brother was a thief," Prichard burst out. "Is that your line as well?"

"Yes, he was and, no, it isn't. I run a charter boat service with the rest of my family in Florida. Wayne didn't like working on boats. Actually, he wasn't all that fond of our family, come to that. Dad was a pretty strict disciplinarian and

Wayne didn't like rules even as a kid. He left after college and in recent years had cut off all communication. But he was still my brother, and he's dead. We want answers and the police haven't been very forthcoming. I was hoping Zoe could help. I didn't anticipate dodging a pair of killers."

Ramsey continued to scrutinize him with dark, assessing eyes. "You seem pretty competent."

"I am." He held the man's gaze. "Let's cut to the chase. Zoe's fiancé is missing and someone wants her dead."

"You know he's missing."

"We spoke to Van Wheeler the same as you must have done."

"Then you know the police would like to talk with Ms. Linden."

Zoe would have spoken, but Xavier silenced her with a light touch on her arm. "The police have already said they can't protect her. Her fiancé appears to have been kidnapped from a secured location. Wayne's partners want something they think she has. The police are going to have to wait."

"How do you know his partners want something from Ms. Linden?"

"I talked to them." It was an effort to curb his growing anger when he thought of the threat to her and to April. He was relieved that Zoe was letting him do the talking. So far she hadn't mentioned his niece, and her controlled expression revealed nothing of what she was thinking, but he was certain she wondered why he wasn't ready to share information on April's kidnapping. Or maybe she realized that as private investigators they might feel obligated to bring in the police.

"I'm scheduled to meet with Wayne's people at seven o'clock tonight. They think I'm going to bring Zoe. I'm not. You run a security firm, right?"

Ramsey inclined his head.

"Then I want to hire you."

Startled, Zoe turned to gape at him. "Xavier!"

"You said you didn't want me going there alone. Despite their performance to date, they can probably take care of themselves and we don't have much time."

Prichard bristled. Ramsey remained cool, at least outwardly. "You should call the police."

"Probably, but I'm not going to. Have you spoken with Trent?"

Ramsey's features tightened.

"That's what I thought. These guys want to make a trade."

"They have Trent?"

"I've no idea, but they said they want to make an exchange. I thought you might want to join me since it would be to your advantage if we could rescue your employer. Easier to collect your bill, for one thing."

"You know what they're looking for?" Ramsey asked.

Xavier nodded toward Holmes, who stood off to one side of the spacious living room in silence. "If your man is correct, they want a briefcase with a fortune in gems and gold."

Ramsey didn't blink. "And you know where this case is?"

"Nope. Frankly, I don't care."

"Ms. Linden?"

"I don't have it. I didn't even know about it until Mr. Holmes mentioned the possibility."

"My brother worked alone for the most part, Ramsey, but I'm pretty sure he took on partners occasionally. The thing is, he had a real dislike for guns. If he *was* part of that robbery, he wouldn't have known they planned to shoot anyone. He'd have walked away if he had."

"You can't know that if you haven't seen him in years."

"I do know that. I didn't approve of what my brother did, but I know him. Robbing people was a game. He loved the challenge. While he was often thoughtless of others, he was never cruel. When the shooting happened, he would have been furious."

"Enough to go to the cops?"

"No. He had his own code of ethics, but I'm guessing his partners didn't share it. They probably saw that possibility as a threat."

Zoe laid a comforting hand on his arm. He covered it with his own. "I don't have a lot of time. I need to get to the rendezvous spot ahead of them and I could use a little help."

The room with its bank of windows had grown progressively darker as the conversation continued. Abruptly, a brilliant flash of light outside drew their gazes to the view. Thick black clouds bubbled across the sky, driven by a wind that shook the building, a grumble of thunder in its wake.

"Right on time."

"I'm impressed." Ramsey arched his eyebrows. "You planned a thunderstorm?"

"I'm not quite that good, but I make use of what I have. I heard it was going to storm and figured that it would make good cover and effectively clear the area of civilians. You willing to help?"

"The police—"

"Would probably get...Harrison killed," Zoe inserted. "No police."

Xavier squeezed her hand in thanks.

"What's your plan?" Ramsey asked.

"Do you think Smiley over there—" he indicated Prichard "—could pass as a woman in the dark from a distance?"

"Not even to a blind man," Eric Holmes responded quickly with a wide grin.

"But *you* might," Ramsey told him, wiping the smile from his face. "What do you have in mind, Drake?"

Chapter Nine

"You promise you won't leave the condo?" Xavier demanded once again.

Zoe knew she would normally feel annoyed, but his obvious concern for her made that impossible. The other three men waited in the foyer by the elevator, out of sight. Zoe smiled and touched his cheek lightly.

"I promise. I'll be fine. Why didn't you tell them about April?"

"Because if they knew a child was involved they'd insist on calling in the police and there isn't time for that now."

"All right. Go find your niece. Then come back and tell me about it."

She'd never known a man who could say so much without opening his lips. He covered her hand with his, and Zoe felt that contact in every pore of her body as he pressed her palm against his roughened jaw.

"You're an incredible woman, Zoe Linden."

A thrill raced through her. He made her feel that way. And when he released her to smooth back a tendril of hair, she wanted to melt in his arms. The thought must have shown, because abruptly he drew her against the solid strength of his body and covered her lips.

Her hips moved reflexively as her body tightened unbearably. She suddenly found herself backed against the wall as his lips took hungry possession of hers in a stirringly sensual kiss that left her breathless and trembling. His leg slid between hers, triggering a flood of passion.

Xavier pulled back, resting his chin on her head. He whispered something that could have been a prayer or a curse as he tried to catch his breath.

"No one has ever turned me on so fast with a mere look." The words electrified her.

"What am I going to do with you?"

She gazed at him, bereft of speech, but wanting to answer with every cell in her body.

"Lock the door behind us. Don't open it to anyone." His voice was gruff and husky, thick with suppressed need. She'd felt the strength of his arousal and knew he was every bit as turned on as she was. Her sensitized breasts ached for his touch.

She raised a troubled gaze to his as he stepped back. Zoe wanted to lead him to the nearest room to finish what they had started but knew that she couldn't.

"Am I locking it against you or the kidnappers?"

"Yes." Xavier shook his head as if to clear it. "I'll be back."

"You'd better be."

He strode toward the hall without looking back.

Zoe stayed against the wall for a long moment before she could bring herself to go to the door and turn the heavy dead bolt. Even then she wasn't entirely steady.

Wayne had swept her off her feet with insane flattery and a suaveness that had been overwhelming, but her captivation had waned almost as quickly as it had formed. Despite his looks and constant attention, it hadn't taken her long to see the other, self-centered side to Wayne that had left her trying to find a tactful way to break off the relationship. Wayne, of course, didn't do tact and she'd had to come right out and tell him she didn't want to see him any longer. Even then, he'd continued to call her.

Xavier was different.

She touched a finger to her still-tingling lips. Very different—and in ways far more fundamental than her sexual response to him. Xavier cared deeply about his family. There was love in his voice every time he mentioned one of them. Not only had Wayne never spoken of his family, he'd never said a word about having a daughter. Zoe couldn't forgive him for that. She tried to picture Wayne charging in to face down April's kidnappers and failed. Xavier would spare nothing to rescue his niece.

Even so, despite her tremendous physical attraction to Xavier, Zoe could not afford to become involved with him. She was already living a genuine soap opera. Not only was she pregnant with Wayne's child, she was still engaged to Harrison.

Harrison! How could she keep forgetting about him? She stared around his expensive living room and wondered if she was going mad. If things had gone as planned, they'd be on their way to Italy right now as husband and wife.

And that would have been a dreadful mistake.

She gazed at the sweeping vista outside his penthouse window and wanted to howl with the storm now raging outside. Harrison was her friend and mentor, and she was going to hurt him by turning down all he had offered her and her child.

Taking a deep breath, she gazed at the opulence of the room. She'd never wanted this. The truth was, this sterile, perfect room had always made her uncomfortable. She wanted a home, not a model penthouse. Somehow, she had to find him to tell him as much.

But Harrison hadn't called her back, and his silence was terrifying. She knew him well. He would never leave her hanging like this. Who was the attractive woman in the car with him? She knew most of his friends. An old girlfriend?

And that didn't even cause a pang. She almost hoped it was true so she wouldn't feel so guilty for the feelings Xavier had stirred in her. Zoe didn't want to hurt Harrison. It was the last thing she wanted. But what had he thought when she hadn't shown up for the wedding?

Artie would have told him she'd cancelled because of his disappearance, yet he'd gone to the church anyhow. If only she could have really talked to him. Why hadn't he called her back?

Zoe watched the dazzling display of lightning setting fire to the heavens, and her thoughts returned to Xavier. She wasn't equipped to deal with armed men in the night, but she hated that he was out there without her while she stood there like some fragile, helpless little woman.

The image sucked. She wasn't fragile and she wasn't helpless. She knew how to make a computer sing, and Harrison had a brand-new machine in his office. If she'd been thinking with her brain instead of reacting with her crazy hormones, she would have realized she could have at least one kidnapper's identity with a few keystrokes. She had the man's telephone number!

DESPITE THE EARLY HOUR, the streets were midnight-black as they raced the storm to the park. Powerful gusts of wind forced rain to batter the world while lightning strobed the landscape in startling snatches of brilliance.

The small park with its brightly colored boats for hire was dark and deserted in the face of the storm. The burned-out shell of the ice-cream stand stood eerily silhouetted against the black water in the flashes of light. The trees surrounding the park and lake whipped to and fro, adding additional menace to the scene.

"We're going to get soaked," Prichard muttered gloomily under his breath.

"You won't melt," Xavier scoffed.

"You sure about this, Drake?"

"That you won't melt? Yeah, I'm sure."

Prichard growled as he adjusted the wig on the blow-up doll in the front seat next to Xavier. "They better show."

"Keep down! We can't be sure we got here first."

"I know my job," the man protested.

"Then do it."

Prichard snarled something as Xavier slowed the car to a crawl. They'd disabled the overhead light, and he leaped from the car and melted away in the dark. Xavier continued on slowly until he reached the empty graveled parking area near the burned-out shell. The rain made it almost impossible to see. That could work against them as easily as for them. It all depended on how badly these men wanted the briefcase.

Prichard had reason to be skeptical. Xavier was far from confident that his plan would work. Originally, he'd planned to sit in the car as bait, but Ramsey had countered that with the blow-up doll and wig he had in the trunk of his car.

"We just used it on a job."

Xavier didn't ask for details. The trunk contained an array of gadgets and equipment that raised his eyebrows, including the weapon now tucked in his waistband. With the blow-up doll as bait, the four men were free to spread out. Xavier planned to draw the killer's focus by walking to the shack, hopefully without being shot. Ramsey, Holmes and Prichard covered the approaches to the parking area.

His breathing steadied and outside thoughts shut down as he focused on the mission. Xavier parked, killed the engine and stepped from the car. This was the critical moment. If the killers were already in position, he could be dead before he reached the building.

Xavier moved with quiet purpose to the side of the ice-cream shack. He was soaked to the skin three steps from the car and blinded by the punishing rain. Lightning sizzled overhead. A barrage of shots came almost immediately from somewhere off to his left, drowned in a violent clap of thunder.

Xavier crouched beside the building. He couldn't tell where the shots had originated. Obviously, they hadn't arrived first. He sidled along the building's length, gun drawn. When he came all the way around without further challenge, he looked toward the car.

Another flash of light showed the shattered passenger side window. He could no longer see the dummy. Cold terror pierced his mind. If they thought they'd killed Zoe…

Xavier broke and ran for the nearest clump of trees. A spate of shots came from Eric Holmes's position. Xavier kept running.

None of them had expected the killers to shoot Zoe first. Xavier should have drawn their initial fire. Zoe had been right. They wanted her dead, and badly enough to leave him in a position to fire back.

They had no use for April now that they thought Zoe was dead. Terror swelled as he ran. He couldn't panic if he wanted to save her. There was still a chance, if they'd brought her with them.

He broke into the open, crossing the parking lot at a dead run. More shots came from the right. Xavier ignored the threat and kept moving. His sodden clothing snagged on wet bushes as he plunged into the trees. He ran on, uncaring of the noise or anything else. He had to locate their car and April.

He'd brought his niece to this park often enough to have a good idea of the layout. Wayne's partners wouldn't risk parking in the trees for fear of getting stuck in the mud. There had been no sign of a vehicle on his way into the park, which meant they were likely stopped along the exit road.

Unless they'd used a residential side street and hiked here in the rain. The thought made his insides twist. He shook it off. They wouldn't risk leaving April unattended that far away. He would not consider that they may have already eliminated her.

Focus on the car. This was Ramsey's quadrant of the park and given the poor visibility, he risked coming under friendly fire. He didn't care.

The stronger gusts were dying down. The sky had lightened some, but the rain continued to fall heavily. What little light there was would soon be gone as the sun began to set.

He was nearly on top of the car before he saw it. Relief flooded him. He'd read them right. The sedan was under the trees a short distance from the end of the parking area.

Heart pounding in anticipation, he forced himself to approach with care. There didn't appear to be anyone inside. The driver's door opened at the touch of his hand. He blinked as the overhead light came on. The men were dumber than he'd thought.

The car was empty, but the idiots had even left the keys in the ignition to make a quicker escape.

Xavier pulled the keys and ran to the trunk. Empty. A rush of despair filled him. They hadn't brought her. If they'd already killed her...

He clamped down hard on the thought. He wouldn't go there. They may have had no intention of making the trade, but they would hold on to April until they'd killed Zoe in case something went wrong. He had to believe that.

He returned to the interior of the car and reached across

the seat for the glove compartment. If they were stupid enough to leave the keys, maybe they'd left the registration as well. A quick search of the car turned up no identification at all.

Pitching the keys in the underbrush, he headed for the hood, intending to yank the distributor cap so they couldn't drive away. Motion in the trees across the road sent him dodging down behind the car wheel. He expected shots. None came.

The person thrashed noisily with no attempt at stealth. Not Ramsey, then, nor one of his people.

When the person passed his position Xavier broke cover and darted across the road. He trailed the sounds, audible even over the rain and distant thunder, staying on the edge of the roadway where he could move more easily.

The person was obviously confused, probably lost under the dark canopy of trees and the driving rain.

"Hold it right there!"

Ramsey's voice stopped them both. Xavier closed the distance while a burst of flame located both people when they traded shots. The person he'd been following suddenly plunged out of the trees, stumbling onto the road in front of him.

Xavier brought him down in a low tackle that carried them both to the asphalt. The person scrambled free. Xavier went after him. This time they landed in a mud puddle with a hard splat.

Lean and wiry, his opponent struggled to bring his gun around. Xavier chopped hard at the wrist holding the weapon. There was a cry as the gun fell from suddenly nerveless fingers. The person continued to thrash, trying to get free. Xavier held on. A ragged fork of lightning revealed the face beneath him.

"Sandy?" He froze.

She got in a hard kick before she stopped struggling as well. "Get off me!"

He rolled off and stood. His arm ached furiously. He suspected he'd opened his wound. When she sat up, he reached to yank her to her feet. Sandy cried out the second he pulled on her gun arm.

"Did I hurt you?" he asked as Ramsey ran up to them.

"I think you broke my wrist."

"Let me see it. What are you doing here?"

Sandy shook her head. Her normally short, impeccably styled honey-blond hair was now a sopping mass plastered flat to her skull. She clutched her wrist against her sodden jacket. "I couldn't sit home and do nothing. I thought I could help."

Xavier swore.

"I take it you know this person?" Ramsey asked.

"Yes. She isn't involved." To Sandy he demanded, "Where did you get the gun?"

"I bought it for protection."

"And nearly blew my head off," Ramsey told her.

"Who are you?"

"Never mind," Xavier interrupted. "We need to get off this road. Their car is back there about fifty feet. It's empty," he added bleakly before she could ask, "but they'll be heading for it. We can't let them leave." He looked at Ramsey. "You okay?"

"It was close, but I'm fine."

They moved to the trees at the edge of the road. "I'll cover the car," Ramsey told him.

"Who are you? Xavier, who is he?"

The sound of an engine revving halted any explanations. Xavier and Ramsey began to run. Tossing the keys hadn't been good enough. He should have figured they either had a second set or would know how to hot-wire a car. Like a fool, he hadn't even noted the license plate number.

The heavy sedan hurtled out of the darkness straight at them. Xavier shoved Sandy toward the trees. He and Ramsey dived for cover a half second too late. Ramsey was a fraction ahead of him and took the brunt of the impact. The thump was audible as the car sped past and they both went down.

Xavier landed hard enough to knock the wind from his lungs and definitely set his arm to bleeding again. Ramsey rolled until he came to a stop at the foot of a tall maple tree.

"Xavier?"

He ignored Sandy, struggling to his feet as soon as he could breathe again. Ramsey was swearing steadily when he reached his side. Running footsteps charged up the road. Xavier whirled to see Holmes and Prichard arriving, guns drawn.

"Mark! You hit?"

"The car bumped him," Xavier explained, unsure which man had spoken.

"They got away?" Prichard demanded.

A wave of despair washed over him. "Did anyone get a plate number?"

Both men shook their heads.

"But I'm pretty sure I tagged one of them," Holmes told him, bending over his boss. "How bad is it, Mark?"

At the same time, Prichard stared behind Xavier. "Who's that?"

Sandy limped toward them.

"She's with me."

"Since when?"

"Since she decided to play kamikaze on her own."

"I'm sorry," she protested, sounding ready to cry. "I thought I could help."

Xavier ignored her. "Get the car. We need to go after them!"

"They're gone, Drake," Prichard told him.

Holmes nodded in agreement. "We aren't going to catch

them now. Terry, get the car and bring it around. Mark's leg is broken."

"Where's your car?" Xavier demanded of Sandy as Prichard set off at a trot.

"In the housing development a few blocks over." She began to cry. "I'm sorry, Xavier. I thought I could help. I couldn't just sit there waiting. She's my daughter."

Holmes jerked to attention. Xavier knew it no longer mattered. They would have to bring the police in now, no matter what Sandy wanted.

"They'll kill her!"

Sandy's panic matched his own, but he shook his head. "Not yet. Not if they still want the briefcase."

Even as he said it, he knew it wasn't true. They'd shot the decoy, so they didn't want Zoe alive. They'd only wanted to draw her out. Now they thought they'd killed her so there was no reason to leave April alive.

"Kill who?" Ramsey demanded. His voice was laced with pain, but even in the dark Xavier felt his gaze. He tried to focus on Ramsey instead of the horror building in his chest.

"My niece. This is Sandy Drake, Wayne's ex-wife. They broke into her house and took her daughter when they couldn't find the briefcase they're looking for."

"So this was never about Trent." His voice was cold.

"Yes and no. I don't know what happened to Trent. Someone took him from the Van Wheeler estate and we assumed it was the same people who took April. But tonight was about getting a seven-year-old girl back to her mother."

"Except they didn't bring her, like you didn't bring Ms. Linden." Holmes shook his head.

"You didn't bring her?" Sandy shrilled.

"It was too risky."

"You risked my daughter for that tramp?"

Prichard arrived with the car, saving Xavier from responding. They spent several pain-filled minutes loading Mark Ramsey inside. Sandy was gone when they'd finished.

"I'll meet you at the hospital," Holmes told Prichard.

"Right."

"Anyone see Sandy leave?" Xavier asked.

"She must have gone back to her car," Holmes told him. "Come on, I'll give you a lift."

Xavier's insides twisted. She'd trusted him and he'd blown it completely. He should have followed his instincts and called in the police from the start.

He clung to the knowledge that April had been alive this afternoon. There was still a chance. There had to be. He had to believe they wouldn't have killed April before they'd made sure of Zoe.

But now they thought they had. They would eliminate her as soon as they got to wherever they were holding her. Xavier wasn't going to get another chance.

Sick with despair and fear, he trotted back to the parking area with Holmes. The storm was moving off, but the rain continued falling steadily.

"How come you weren't straight with us?" Holmes asked.

"You would have insisted on calling in the cops. I promised Sandy I wouldn't."

"Stupid."

Xavier wiped at his face and realized not all the moisture was rain.

"What about Ms. Linden?" Holmes continued.

"What about her?"

"I take it she knows about the kid?"

"That's why she went along. We don't know what happened to Trent."

"You know Ramsey is going to report this as soon as he gets to the hospital."

Xavier shrugged. What did it matter? None of it mattered anymore. Sandy didn't know the dummy had been shot, so she wouldn't realize how bad the situation was now. He thought about telling her and knew he couldn't. Irrationally, Zoe was the one he wanted to tell.

"I need to pick up my car."

Holmes frowned. Xavier eyed the shattered car window and the bullet holes in the side. His insides lurched painfully.

"Decent shooting," Holmes pointed out as he slid behind the wheel and tossed the destroyed blow-up doll in the backseat. "Especially under these conditions."

Sick despair filled his mind.

"He must have been close to the car. Probably by that path leading down to the dock. The angle is about right. You okay? Were you hurt when the car hit you?"

Was he? Xavier couldn't feel anything. He kept seeing April's bright young face.

"I need to pick up my rental car."

Holmes frowned. "You're going to have to talk to the cops, you know."

"I'm going to check on Zoe first."

Xavier rubbed at his eyes. The other man's sudden silence was pregnant with unspoken words. "What?"

"You do know the lady was supposed to get married today?" Holmes asked without inflection.

"So?"

Holmes shrugged. "Ms. Linden will be fine as long as she doesn't let anyone up to the penthouse. The security there is tight. And Mark has an operative covering the place."

He hadn't known that.

"We were hired to guard Ms. Linden and until we hear different, that's what we intend to do."

Xavier managed a nod. He rubbed his face with both hands. He needed to see Zoe. She'd understand the grief and fear tearing him apart inside. He wanted to hold her close and feel the reality of her. It could so easily have been her head instead of a dummy's tonight. And April…

Holmes cast a sideways glance at him. "You gonna let this get messy?"

"What?"

"Ms. Linden."

For a moment, he didn't understand, and then he did. Anger turned his words harsh. "My niece is probably dead. It's my fault. How much messier do you think it can get?"

Absently, he pressed against his upper arm to stem the bleeding. His hip began to ache where the fender had grazed him and he almost welcomed the distraction. They drove the rest of the way in silence. Despite his muddy, bedraggled appearance no one in the mostly empty parking garage gave him a second glance as he got in and started the engine. He pulled out automatically, not knowing or caring if Holmes followed him.

He was nearing Trent's condo when it hit him like a thunderbolt. He didn't have the phone number for Trent, but he *did* have the number for the killers. He nearly sideswiped a van in his rush to pull out his cell phone.

"Pick up. Pick up!" His hand shook visibly as he waited for someone to answer.

A machine finally responded. A familiar gruff voice told him to leave a message.

"This is Xavier Drake. You shot a blow-up doll tonight, not Zoe. You hear me, you bastard? Zoe is very much alive. Call me the minute you get this message or I promise you will never see that briefcase or its contents." He repeated his cell-phone number and disconnected.

He parked in the fire lane in front of Trent's building and strode inside. His grim features dared anyone to question his right to be there.

The man behind the desk was good. His eyes widened a fraction, but his face remained impassive as Xavier stood there dripping mud and water on the pristine floor.

"May I help you, sir?"

"Harrison Trent's penthouse. The name is Xavier Drake."

"One moment, sir." He didn't take his eyes from Xavier as he reached for a phone and buzzed the suite. After several seconds he shook his head. "I'm sorry, sir, there's no answer."

Xavier's stomach went into free fall. They couldn't have gotten Zoe, too. Please, God, he couldn't take it if she was dead as well.

The door to the hall leading to the elevators suddenly opened and Zoe came striding out. Dressed in a dark wind-breaker, she clutched an umbrella in one hand and a sheaf of papers in the other. She blinked in shock when she registered his presence.

"Xavier!" Zoe ran to him.

He hadn't known he was holding his breath until she flung herself at him. It was too much. He shut eyes filled with moisture.

"What happened?"

"They didn't bring her." He could barely say the thick words.

"Then let's go get her."

His eyes jerked open.

"I know where they are."

Chapter Ten

"Is your car out front?" Zoe added quickly. Grief and anguish were in Xavier's voice and every line of his body. Aware of their audience, Zoe took his wet, muddy arm and steered him back toward the front door.

"What do you mean you know where they are?"

"I wasn't sitting on my hands while you were gone. I used their phone number to track them down on the Internet. Well, one of them, anyhow. His name is Simon Schlosky. Is your suitcase still in the trunk? Give me the keys. I'll drive while you change out of those wet clothes in the backseat. I have the directions." She wiggled the printout. "I was going to leave them for you at the desk with the night man in case you got back before I did."

"You were going to go over there? Alone?"

"Relax, I was only going to scope the place out. I wasn't going to do anything. I figured it would be perfectly safe. The bad guys were with you, after all."

"Zoe—"

"Yell at me later. If they didn't bring her with them I assume we don't have much time. Open the trunk, Xavier."

He opened the trunk and she took the car keys as he lifted his suitcase out.

"Drive fast," he admonished. "They think you're dead so they don't need April anymore. We don't have any time left."

"Why do they think I'm dead? What happened?"

Zoe got behind the wheel, ignoring the damp seat. Xavier looked awful and his panic was contagious. Whatever had happened tonight had been bad.

"Ramsey set a rubber dummy on the seat so they'd think I had you in the car. Someone shot it through the head."

Shocked, her gaze flashed to the rearview mirror. He was pulling his muddy, sopping wet shirt over his head. Blood stained his bandaged arm. She yanked her gaze from his muscled chest and tried to ignore the rustling sounds at her back as he undressed.

"Your arm's bleeding again."

"It'll stop."

Tension underscored each word as he related what had happened at the park. Fear knotted her belly. "Poor Sandy." Zoe couldn't imagine what the woman was going through right now. "You just let her go home alone?"

"She left while we were getting Ramsey in the car. Can you go any faster?"

"Not without causing a wreck. We should be there in a couple of minutes." But she edged up the speed a couple more notches.

"Simon Schlosky owns a town house in Reston," she told him. "He's married with two daughters and works for a lawn company."

"You got all that off the Internet?"

"You can get just about anything off the Internet if you know where to look. The phone number gave me his name and address so I ran a search on the last name. Turns out his wife has a Web page because she makes and sells quilts. She included family photos right down to the dog they no longer have. Her blog mentions him, before you ask. People will put anything on Web sites, but there's no question that the man in the family shots is one of the men we saw on the stairs the other night."

Simon Schlosky had looked like an average family man in those photos, not a cold-blooded killer. Yet he and his partner had tried to put a bullet through her head twice now. And as hard as that was to believe, she simply couldn't accept that with two daughters of his own he could kill an innocent child.

"Pull over," Xavier demanded abruptly.

"Why? We're almost there." And it was amazing that she hadn't wrecked the car or been picked up for speeding.

Xavier leaned between the seats. He'd donned a dark-hued T-shirt and was shrugging into a lightweight jacket.

"I don't want you anywhere near this guy."

"Me, either. I don't have a death wish, Xavier."

"Then what are you doing?"

What *was* she doing, racing to a killer's front door? "Thinking with my emotions, not my head," she admitted wryly. "We need to call the police."

"There wasn't time before and there sure isn't time now. It may already be too late."

"That's exhaustion talking. Schlosky has a wife and two children. He's not going to kill April in front of them."

"He won't have stashed her at his place."

His anguish was overpowering.

"Then I have nothing to worry about if we just drive past the house. We need a starting place, Xavier. That has to be his development up ahead on the left. Besides, it's pouring rain out here. I'd prefer not to get soaked standing on some street corner while you go talk to his wife. Face it, this is the last place he'll expect me to be."

Besides which, this man had made her live in fear for weeks. Zoe wanted to see where he lived.

"All right. Pull into the development, drive past his unit and stop so we can change places."

"No problem."

The address proved to be an end-unit town house with a deserted look to it. No light gleamed anywhere inside. The tiny patch of lawn was badly in need of attention. The units had attached garages so there was no way to tell if someone was inside or not because the minuscule driveway was empty. So was the other parking space allocated to his address.

In the distance, more lightning streaked across the sky. Zoe parked in an empty parking space and pulled out her cell phone.

"What are you doing?"

"Calling his house. Everything's dark. Let's find out if anyone is home. I can always say I misdialed."

Xavier didn't object, but waited tensely. After four rings the answering machine picked up and a man's voice told her to leave a message.

"Looks like there's no one home."

"Wait here." Xavier stepped out of the car before she could ask him his plan.

Zoe held her breath when he headed straight for the house. To her consternation, he walked up and rang the front doorbell. Fear lanced through her. He stood in plain sight and waited.

Nothing happened beyond a brilliant fork of lightning that made her jump. Another storm arrived on a grumble of thunder. Xavier left the front door and started around the town house. Zoe gripped the steering wheel and stared at the silent structure. Her heart raced in her chest as the seconds passed. Surely he wouldn't break in.

Of course he was going to break in. This was Xavier. He'd do anything to save his niece even if it meant breaking the law in the process.

A small face appeared in the darkened window of what was

probably a corner bedroom on the second floor. Zoe was out of the car and running before there was time to think.

Pulling her hood tightly closed, she ignored the slashing rain and raced around the town house after Xavier. He was climbing over the fence that enclosed the tiny backyard.

"Xavier, wait!"

Her call was too late. He'd leaped inside the enclosure out of sight. Zoe was debating what to do when a second later, he opened the gate to her.

"Get back in the car!"

She wiped at the rain streaming down her face. "There's someone inside the house. I think it's a little girl. I saw her face in an upstairs window."

Xavier turned without a word. She followed him inside the enclosure. He tried the sliding glass door beneath the small deck. It didn't budge. Climbing on the fence, he used it to reach up and pull himself onto the deck above. He did it so fast there wasn't time to blink. Zoe drew in a sharp breath as she heard the door up there slide open.

She didn't let herself think. She grabbed the fence and attempted to duplicate his actions.

"What do you think you're doing?" Xavier snapped as he reached out, grabbed her arm and pulled her up and over the railing without effort.

"Getting in out of the rain," she panted.

He startled her by hugging her close for a second.

"Did you forget you're pregnant?"

Actually, she had, but she realized his angry tone was to cover the fear he'd felt for her. She managed a smile. "Maybe she'll turn out to be an Olympic gymnast."

Xavier shook his head, released her and turned back to the door.

"Schlosky has daughters, remember?" she whispered. "It

might have been one of them. If so, she'll be scared to death to have a strange man breaking into her house."

"And you think she'll be okay with a strange woman?" Shaking his head, he started to step inside. "Don't make any noise."

"I sent the marching band home," she whispered back.

While tension clawed at him, Zoe's weak attempts at humor helped hold Xavier's panic at bay. She'd scared him, climbing up on the fence that way. She could have been hurt, but nothing seemed to faze her. He wondered if she'd feel differently if they got caught inside and April wasn't there. The police would view their presence as illegal entry. She should have waited in the car.

The rapid flashes of lightning gave him the lay of the rooms as he paused inside the kitchen. Thunder covered what little sounds they made, but Zoe had been right about one thing—he didn't like the possibility he might terrify some innocent child.

Xavier listened hard. The only sound came from the ticking of a large wall clock. Absently he noted dishes, silverware and glasses piled on the sink. An empty pizza box lay open on the counter. The trash can overflowed with fast-food wrappers.

Either Mrs. Schlosky didn't like to cook and clean or she wasn't home and hadn't been for a while. It gave him hope. There were no lights on in the house, but the power was obviously working. Numbers glowed on the microwave.

Xavier moved quickly through the dining area and living room. Newspapers littered the table along with forgotten plates and more glasses. A pair of men's shoes sat in front of a recliner in the living room along with several empty beer bottles and a couple of glasses.

Zoe made no sound as she trailed behind him. His adrenaline pumped as he mounted the steep stairs. The narrow hall opened onto three doors. Two of them gaped open. Zoe tapped his arm to indicate the closed room on his left.

As soon as he saw the bolt someone had installed on the outside of the door he knew. He was shaking as he opened it. "April?"

The small form hurtled across the dark room and threw herself at him, wrapping her arms fiercely around his waist. "Uncle Xavier!"

As he swallowed convulsively, tears mingled with the moisture dripping from his wet hair. He lifted her in his arms, pressing her tightly to his chest. "I got you, baby. It's okay. It's okay. Are you all right?"

She nodded against his chest. Her arms twined tightly around his neck as she trembled violently. "What took you so long?"

Zoe made a strangled sound. Xavier thought there were tears in her eyes as she watched them.

"Who's she?" April demanded, suddenly fearful.

"This is Zoe. She helped me find you."

"Oh. Can we go home now?"

"Right now," he promised.

Zoe turned and led the way back down the stairs, wiping at her eyes. Xavier stopped her when she started to turn back toward the kitchen. "We're going out the front door."

"Okay, but she'll need a coat. It's pouring out there."

"I don't care," April asserted. "I'm already wet from Uncle Xavier. I just want to go home."

"We're going home, baby. I promise."

Only a single jacket hung in the narrow closet by the front door. Zoe covered the girl with it while Xavier opened the door. When Zoe would have closed it behind them, he shook his head. "Leave it."

Her expression showed her understanding. He wanted to

make a statement. The minute the bastard returned, he wanted Schlosky to know it was over.

"I'll drive if you want to ride in back with her," Zoe offered.

"Thanks."

They sprinted for the car. He had to put his suitcase and wet clothes in the trunk first to make room in the backseat.

"Are you sure you're okay, April?" Zoe asked her.

"Uh-huh."

"And they didn't hurt you?" Xavier demanded again, getting in beside her.

"No. I was scared, but they just locked me in that room and told me if I wasn't good they'd hurt Mom. They didn't, did they? I tried to be good."

Xavier held her tight, stroking her hair as she shivered against him. "Your mom's fine. She's been terribly worried about you."

She nodded against his side. "Can me and Mom go to Florida with you now, Uncle Xavier?"

"If your mom is okay with it, we'll get the first plane out in the morning," he promised. He met Zoe's understanding gaze in the mirror.

"Is Zoe your girlfriend, Uncle Xavier?"

Zoe answered before he could decide what to say. "Your uncle has been helping me while we were looking for you."

"Oh. Thank you for finding me."

"You're welcome. I'm glad the men didn't hurt you."

"Only at first when they tied me up. I tried to do what you said when someone tries to grab me, Uncle Xavier, but I screamed and kicked and they wouldn't let me go. They were too strong. They were in our house when Sara's mom dropped me off. The bigger one grabbed me when I tried to run and covered my mouth. He was mean, but his brother told him not to hurt me."

His hands fisted impotently, even as Xavier jumped on that last. "His brother?"

April nodded. "He said, 'You might be my brother, but I won't let you hurt her. She's just a kid.'"

Xavier and Zoe exchanged looks.

"The mean one said I'd seen their faces and they'd go to jail. I said I wouldn't tell anyone, but he wouldn't listen. He wanted to know where my dad put some briefcase. I told him Daddy was dead and didn't have a briefcase, but he wouldn't listen."

"It's okay, April."

"They tied me up at first, but then Simon bought a lock for the outside of the door so he could untie me. He said it was his daughter's room."

"You didn't see his daughter?"

"She doesn't live there anymore. They're getting a divorce like Mom and Dad. The men were yelling at each other yesterday and the mean one said Simon was stupid and that's why his wife took his daughters and left. He wanted to get rid of me, but Simon said once they found the case it wouldn't matter what I told the police because they could disappear. I was scared they'd find the case and go away and leave me there."

Xavier hugged her more tightly.

"When you called, I knew you would find me even though the mean one wouldn't let me talk to you."

Xavier throttled back his rage as he stroked her hair. Once again he met Zoe's warm gaze. Her silent support steadied him.

"Are you hungry, April?" Zoe asked. "I can stop at a drive-through and get you something to eat."

"No. Simon brought me pizza. He was always buying me hamburgers and stuff to eat. It was boring. There wasn't anything to do. There were some books and a few toys in the closet, but they were mostly baby things and I could only read when it was bright outside. The room didn't have a light or a computer or a television or anything."

"I'll make it up to you," Xavier promised, relieved that was the extent of April's complaints.

Zoe caught his eye. "I need directions to her mom's place."

Xavier allowed the tension of the past few weeks to trickle away as they drove to Sandy's house. Whatever happened, April was safe and he was going to see that she stayed that way.

His stomach knotted again when he spotted two unmarked police cars in front of Sandy's house. Apparently, Ramsey hadn't wasted any time notifying them.

"Maybe you should drop us and go," Xavier suggested.

Zoe shook her head. "We're in this together."

"We broke a few laws."

She shrugged that off. "I know a good lawyer. The important thing is we got April back and no one got hurt."

He loved this woman. And that was a very scary thought. "We still don't know what happened to Trent."

Her expression clouded. "One step at a time. Should I call Carter Hughes before we go inside?"

It took him a moment to remember that was the name of Trent's lawyer. "Let's wait and see if we need him, first. Let me do most of the talking."

She smiled. "I'm just a helpless little woman."

Xavier grinned. "My sisters are going to love you."

They started toward the front door and she laid a warm hand on his arm.

"Just a suggestion, but I'd tell them you came to see me about your brother." Zoe's voice became fast and urgent. "Two men started chasing us and even broke down an apartment door looking for us." Her eyes gleamed in the porch light. "I'm fine with skimming details."

"You're fine in every way."

Her lips parted. April suddenly broke free and ran to open the front door. She burst inside with a loud cry. "Mommy!"

Three plainclothes police officers looked up. Sandy's tear-filled eyes widened in shock. "April?"

Xavier didn't know when he put his arm around Zoe, but it felt completely natural as they watched the tearful reunion. He drew her against his side, oddly at peace for the first time since his brother's death. Zoe laid her head against his wet shoulder. She was wiping at her eyes again.

"Mr. Drake?" one of the officers asked.

"Yes."

The man regarded Zoe. "And you are?"

"Zoe Linden."

"Linden?" The three people exchanged glances of surprise. "Would you folks like to step into the kitchen with me?"

"Not really," Zoe answered.

Xavier hid a smile. No one intimidated his Zoe.

"It would be appreciated, ma'am."

Xavier steered her toward the kitchen. "I could really use a cup of hot coffee."

"Personally, I wonder if there's any chance of some peanut butter cookies."

THE POLICE WERE NOT happy. They did let Zoe rebandage Xavier's bleeding arm and even offered him medical attention, which he refused. She remained mostly mute, letting Xavier answer their questions. He, in turn, pared those answers to their simplest components, sticking with the truth as much as possible.

Eventually, Sandy came in and asked Xavier to carry a sleeping April to her bed for the night.

"My wrist is bothering me."

Xavier frowned. "I'm sorry, Sandy. You should have someone look at it."

"It will be okay. It's just sore."

Neither of them explained what was wrong with her wrist and the police officers moved away, leaving Zoe to face Sandy alone for the first time. That Sandy disliked her was apparent from her sour expression.

"Xavier says he couldn't have rescued April without your help. Thank you."

Obviously, the brittle words cost her. Zoe felt bad. She *had* been the other woman in Wayne's life if only briefly and all unknowingly. "I'm glad I could help."

Sandy turned away stiffly and followed Xavier and April upstairs. Zoe sank back against the kitchen chair and closed her eyes, letting exhaustion sweep over her.

Xavier found her there when he finally made his way back to the kitchen. He touched her shoulder tenderly, hating to wake her even to take her home, but she opened her eyes immediately.

"Ready to go?"

"They're letting us leave?"

"With the understanding we hold ourselves available for further questioning."

Zoe groaned and stood.

"I hope it's okay with you that I told them they could reach us at Trent's place. They're going to keep a police presence here for the reminder of the night, but they have a pickup order out for the Schlosky brothers. The detective doesn't think there will be any more trouble tonight."

"Good." Zoe handed him the keys. "You can drive. I'm too tired."

She climbed into the passenger's side and sat there with her eyes closed. Her features were too pale. She needed sleep and so did he, although he was so wound up he wasn't sure he *could* sleep. His shoulder competed with his hip for attention, and even muscles used to hard work were protesting the day's abuses.

"How can they have more questions?" she asked as they approached the penthouse. Her voice was thick with fatigue.

"They're cops. It's what they do. Don't worry, we'll deal." He used her pass card to park under the building and lifted her suitcase from the car.

"You'll need yours, too," she told him with a yawn.

Tired, damp and bedraggled, she still made his pulses race. "I can't stay." The words came out more gruffly than he'd intended.

She brushed that aside with a wave of her hand. "Of course you can. Harrison has a spare bedroom and it's too late to hunt for a motel. Besides, you told the police this was where we were going."

"It doesn't feel right."

"Get over it, Xavier. I'm too tired to argue with you."

They shared a yawn. The adrenaline rush had faded. He was ready to hibernate for a month. But as he looked at her delicate features, the part of him that wasn't tired was disconcerted. Given the thoughts he'd been having about Zoe, he wasn't comfortable staying in her fiancé's condo.

"Xavier, please. Let's not argue over this. I don't want to stay here alone tonight."

She knew which button to push. Reluctantly, he removed his suitcase as well.

"You may have to carry me off this elevator," Zoe announced a few minutes later. "I can't believe I can be this tired and still stand. I am still standing, aren't I?"

"For the moment," he agreed, wanting nothing more than to gather her in his arms.

Her eyes drifted closed. He gripped the suitcases more tightly so he wouldn't be tempted to reach out and touch her. She swayed slightly as the elevator glided to a stop and the doors parted. Xavier didn't trust himself to steady her. He was glad for the suitcases filling his hands with something other than her.

She unlocked the foyer door and held it open. "If you want anything, food, drinks…"

You was on the tip of his tongue, yearning to be inserted.

"…whatever, help yourself."

She had no idea how tempting that offer was.

"It really is okay. Harrison won't mind."

Oh, Xavier thought, *Harrison Trent would mind very much, indeed.*

She tilted her head, suddenly gazing up at him. "What?"

"I'm good." Even if it killed him.

"I can't argue with that."

And if she kept looking at him like that it just might.

She hesitated. Maybe it was wishful thinking, but he thought he glimpsed a responding flash of sensual awareness in her eyes before she turned away briskly.

"Come on, I'll show you the spare room."

Xavier was in a dangerous frame of mind and he knew exactly why. April was safe. Now he was free to acknowledge the temptation Zoe had presented from the first time he'd laid eyes on her. He wanted her.

It didn't matter that it was a bad idea. He didn't care that she was engaged or that she carried his brother's child. Nothing mattered but the desire humming through his veins.

Letting her show him to a bed seemed like a very bad idea.

"This is fine, Zoe. I'll sack out on the couch down here."

"Don't be silly. Come on."

She didn't look at him. That was a good thing. She might have seen the hunger clamoring to be free. He followed the slight sway of her hips up the stairs, mentally trying to remember the coordinates to some of his favorite tourist fishing spots. He couldn't remember any of them.

The spare room was spacious, neat and airy, with another great view of the city's rain-drenched lights. Xavier couldn't have cared less. He no longer felt sleepy. He ran a hand over his face, feeling the trace of bristles along his jaw.

"I can take my own suitcase the rest of the way," she told him. "Get some rest, Xavier."

His body said rest could come later. His conscience told him he should be a gentleman and carry her suitcase for her. But if he wanted to stay a gentleman…

He set it down so he wouldn't inadvertently touch her hand. Touching her would be fatal. April was safe and euphoria filled him. Zoe was anything but safe. He'd let her carry her own suitcase.

"Thank you, Zoe." The words came from his heart. "Without you, April could have died tonight."

The warmth of her answering smile caused a hitch in his breathing.

"I'm so glad it turned out all right."

"So am I."

Their gazes locked.

Zoe couldn't catch her breath. The naked longing in his eyes called to her so strongly she found herself leaning in his direction. If he touched her now…

Somehow, she found her voice. "Good night, Xavier." And the strength to walk away. She knew he watched her go. If only things were different.

What was wrong with her? Pregnancy might be screwing with her hormones, but she wasn't the sort of person who went from one man to another, despite how her life must look to an outsider right now. But Xavier was…

…everything she'd ever wanted?

Zoe shut her eyes tightly against the thought. She opened them quickly and looked at the mess they'd made on the bed in the room Harrison had given her. No way. She was far too tired to clear this up right now. While tempted to drop her case, shove stuff aside and curl up on the edge of the bed, common sense told her she was being ridiculous. Harrison wasn't here. There was no reason she couldn't spend the night in his bed. If the wedding had gone off as planned...

But it hadn't, and Zoe was relieved. "And I'm far too tired for foolish thoughts," she whispered sternly.

She strode across the hall to his room, set her suitcase down and pulled out the items she would need for the night. She'd packed for a honeymoon in Italy. Fortunately, her tastes didn't run to frilly nightgowns or she'd have to go back to her room and pull out her old sleeping jersey. The pale peach gown she removed from the suitcase was satin soft and delicate, but not provocative.

Not that Xavier would see her in it, anyhow. She lifted out the matching robe and stepped into Harrison's huge bathroom. Her breathing came to a dead stop.

The sink was wet.

How could the sink be wet? Her gaze fell on the crumpled, damp hand towel. Fear's icy fingers traveled down her spine. Someone had been in here.

Zoe ran to the guest room. Finding it empty, she burst through the open bathroom door. "Someone's in here!"

Only then did she realize Xavier was unfastening the button on his waistband. His chest and feet were bare. He was preparing to take a shower.

"Where?" He tugged her away from the door and stepped between her and the opening.

Her teeth began to chatter. "I don't know. Someone used the sink in Harrison's bathroom. The towel is still damp."

"Wait here."

He strode from the room. Zoe followed on his heels. It had

to be Harrison. It was his bathroom, his penthouse. Why was she so panicked?

Because Harrison would think Xavier was an intruder!

"Xavier! Wait!"

He was already moving into Harrison's bathroom.

"It must have been Harrison. Maybe Leon."

"Who else has key cards to this place?"

"Harrison, Leon and I are the only ones I know of."

"What about Van Wheeler?"

Zoe hesitated. "I'm not sure."

"I suppose it's a waste of breath to ask you to wait here while I check the rest of the place."

"If it's Harrison, he'll think you're a burglar!"

Xavier scowled. "Stay behind me."

He crossed to her room and studied the bed. "I can't be sure, but I think I closed that briefcase and left it on the dresser over there when we were looking through your things earlier."

The case sat open on the bed.

"I don't remember."

"Where's the ring box?"

She stared at him blankly.

"I set that on the end of the bed. Unless you picked it up?"

She shook her head, surveying the mess. The ring box was missing.

With a terse nod, he checked every inch of the room before moving on. In the greenhouse he paused to lift a broken stem from the floor. The leaf attached was still green and fresh.

Silently, she stepped forward to show him how to turn on the lights outside. The pool area was empty. The doors leading outside were closed and locked from the inside. There was no other way down from the roof.

Her heart continued to race as they moved through the rest

of the penthouse without speaking. There was no one else in the place. Xavier led the way back to the kitchen. His sun-bronzed skin gleamed in the artificial light. Well-toned muscles rippled with tension. The tape on his injured arm stood out in sharp contrast.

"Would the front desk know if Trent had come in tonight?"

"Probably. They monitor the garage with cameras. Do you want me to call down and ask?"

He glanced at the clock on the wall and shook his head. "I don't think so. We don't want to raise a lot of questions at this hour."

"Why not?"

"Because it may have been one of Ramsey's people."

"How would he get in? And why? They're working for Harrison, not spying on him."

"True."

"And why would one of his people take the ring?"

That he couldn't explain. "You're right. Most likely, it was Trent."

"Then where is he?"

"We need to get out of here."

"And go where?"

Exhaustion lined his mouth and eyes. "We'll find a motel."

"Right. Because that would be so much safer than staying here in a secured building."

He ignored her sarcasm. "It's not so secure if someone got in here once already tonight. Are you trying to convince me or yourself?"

"Xavier, it couldn't have been the Schloskys. There's no way I'll believe that."

"No, they wouldn't have had time unless they split up tonight. Although, that's possible. We have no way of knowing how many people were in those woods."

"Say one of them did break in. How is a motel going to be any safer than staying here? Do you think they'll come back?"

Xavier rubbed his jaw tiredly. "No. Okay. I want you to sleep with me tonight."

She forgot to take a breath. "I beg your pardon?"

Xavier swore. He was pretty sure he hadn't blushed since he was nine or ten years old. "I meant I want you to sleep in the same room with me."

Was that disappointment? The expression was gone in an instant as Zoe cleared her throat.

"That's what I thought you meant."

For a second, he almost said something else before sanity reasserted itself. "Zoe, if someone got in here once, they can do it again. I don't want them finding you alone. You can take the bed and I'll take the floor in front of the door."

"That's a bit extreme."

"Think so? Tell me you're comfortable sleeping alone tonight."

"Not anymore," she admitted.

"Okay then."

"All the beds are king-size, Xavier. We can share like we did the other night. You don't need to sleep on the floor."

"Yeah," he told her. "I do."

The room seemed to shrink. Her gaze slid across his bare chest to trace the fine hairs dipping below his unbuttoned waistband. Her eyes widened as she took in the arousal beginning to press against the fabric.

"Oh." Color stained her cheeks.

"Yeah. Oh. But don't worry, I'm not going to lose control and jump you."

"Well, darn." Her eyes came up to meet his. "How about if *I* jump *you?*"

Chapter Eleven

Molten heat flooded his veins. As soon as the words left her lips, Xavier realized two things: she wanted him, and taking her tonight would be a huge mistake. Zoe had already made two mistakes with the men in her life. Xavier didn't want to be number three. He was pretty sure if he took her to bed now, he'd never be able to walk away and she wasn't ready for that. She might never be ready for what he wanted from her.

"I wouldn't say no, Zoe, but the timing's all wrong, don't you think?"

Her relief was palpable. "If things were different…"

"Yes."

She closed her eyes, inhaled and opened them again immediately. "You're a good man, Xavier Drake."

When she would have touched his face he drew back. "Not that good. Go upstairs and finish getting ready for bed. We'll use the guest room."

He kept his gaze firmly on each tread as he followed her up the stairs and tried not to imagine the two of them entwined on the bed up there. Xavier waited while she gathered her things and carried them into the spare room.

"You can use the bathroom first."

She started to speak, changed her mind and closed the

bathroom door behind her. His imagination supplied the details when he heard the shower come on. He worked off his tension by moving the heavy walnut dresser in front of the bedroom door before starting his evening exercise routine.

When Zoe exited the room on a waft of fragrant steam, her cheeks were flushed and dewy. Her damp hair was wrapped in a towel and an utterly feminine slinky peach robe fell like satin over her curves. His body responded instantly.

She didn't look at him. Instead, she took in the dresser and cocked her head. "Isn't that a bit extreme?"

"Not if someone tries to come in while I'm in the shower."

"Oh."

Her gaze drifted to him. He rubbed a hand over the bristles on his jaw as it moved to the pillow and blanket he'd set on the floor. He didn't wait for her to comment, but headed into the bathroom.

Xavier took his time. He emerged to find Zoe asleep, curled tightly on the edge of the far side of the bed. Her cheeks were puffy and tear-stained, making his heart ache. The pillow and blanket he'd put on the floor now lay like a gauntlet on the bed.

He swore softly. "I'm sorry," he whispered, not even sure what he was apologizing for.

He wished Trent would show up. He had some choice words to say to the rich bastard.

SUNSHINE TICKLED HIM awake a short time after dawn. Xavier was used to going with little sleep, so he rose and dressed quietly. He folded the blanket and moved the dresser back into place without waking Zoe. She looked like a fairy-tale princess with all the stress smoothed from her features. It was all he could do not to lean over and kiss her awake.

Instead, he prowled the penthouse. Nothing had changed

overnight. Whoever had been inside hadn't returned. Still, he longed to be gone as quickly as possible.

Xavier discovered one perk. Harrison Trent stocked the best-tasting coffee he'd ever had. There was little in the way of perishables to eat, but the freezer held steaks and bread and the pantry even yielded a small jar of peanut butter. Zoe would survive.

He was watching CNN on his third cup of coffee when she entered the kitchen, looking crisp and cool in a mint-green blouse and summery skirt.

"I'd kill for a cup of that," she announced.

"Not necessary. I promise there's plenty."

There was no sign of unease or discomfort as she faced him. He wondered if she knew he'd slept on the bed with her.

"I wish. I'm off caffeine until after the baby is born."

"Oh. I have a couple of steaks warming in the oven and I defrosted a loaf of bread."

"Leon's homemade bread? Yum. And peanut butter!"

"Yea-a-ah…if you don't mind, I'd rather not watch you put that on your steak again. I'm going to have nightmares as it is."

"Wimp." She began rummaging through the neatly organized pantry. "I know Leon keeps decaffeinated tea in here somewhere. Ah, here we go. Have you spoken to April this morning?"

"It's still early yet."

He curbed his impatience to be away and they worked comfortably together, setting out plates and slicing bread. He could get used to a morning routine like this one. And he really wished he could stop having thoughts like that. If his engagement to Kath had shown him anything, it was that life was all about making the right choices. A woman who preferred a pampered environment like this one wasn't the right woman for him no matter how much his emotions wanted it otherwise.

In deference to him, Zoe settled for slathering the toast with peanut butter and not the steak. He waited until she was mostly finished before broaching the topic he wanted to discuss.

"I think you should fly to Florida with us."

Zoe stopped chewing. She eyed him thoughtfully.

"I know this is your home, but until those men are in custody, you aren't safe here. The police can't protect you. They said as much. And no matter how good he thinks his people are, neither can Ramsey. I told you my family runs a charter boat service. No one can get to you on the open water."

"You want me to go sailing with you?"

"Not just me. We'll take April and Sandy and a couple of the older kids. Believe me, with that crew on board your virtue will be perfectly safe and it will give the police time to clean up at this end. You already have the time off." He wished he hadn't reminded her of the aborted wedding, but she didn't look upset. In fact, she was almost smiling.

"I wasn't worried about my virtue, Xavier, but what about Harrison?"

The major stumbling block.

He'd known it would come down to the other man. "I think Trent can look after himself, don't you? He never bothered calling you back."

He ignored the flash of pain and drove his point home. "You're in danger. Whatever happened to Trent, he isn't around to protect you right now. The two of you can resolve your relationship issues when you get back."

"He must be in some sort of trouble."

"What are you going to do to fix it if he is?"

She took a sip of tea. Her hand was steady. She regarded him calmly. "There's nothing I can do for him."

"Exactly."

She took a final bite of toast, chewed and swallowed.

"Did I mention I know a little something about boats?"

Xavier blinked in surprise.

"I grew up in the Annapolis area and Dad used to take us out in the bay all the time. We owned a small pleasure boat, and it was a lot of fun. I haven't been sailing in a long time."

The other arguments he'd spent the morning marshalling faded away. She was going to come with him.

"You'll like my family. They'll spoil you rotten."

Her smile hit him in the solar plexus.

"All I need is a bathing suit. I wasn't taking one to Italy."

He tried to brake his building excitement. "They sell bathing suits in Florida."

"I'm pregnant."

He was smiling. "We even have pregnant women in Florida."

"I'm sure you do. I'll need a couple of minutes to repack."

"Can I help?"

She smiled serenely. "I can manage. Thanks."

Xavier's pleasure faded once they finally entered the elevator to go to the parking garage. If an attack came, it would be when the doors opened at the garage level. He made Zoe stand behind him as they came to a stop, but like every other time he'd been down there it was eerily silent. They could have been the only people in the building. Still, he didn't relax until they were on their way to Sandy's.

He was almost relieved when they picked up a tail the moment they pulled out of the garage. Xavier recognized Eric Holmes's car right away. He'd come to like and respect the older detective and he welcomed the man's presence at their backs.

It disturbed him that he didn't see the expected police car out front when he pulled up at Sandy's.

"Eric Holmes followed us here," he told Zoe. "I want a quick word with him before we go inside."

"I'll wait in the car."

He hesitated, but Sandy resented Zoe so he nodded. "I'll just be a minute."

Holmes had parked three houses down. The man rolled down the passenger window at Xavier's approach.

"How's Ramsey?"

"Compound fracture," Holmes replied. "He's cursing a blue streak, but he'll be fine. Our man lost you last night."

"We got April back."

"So I heard. Congratulations."

"Was it one of your people inside the penthouse yesterday?"

Eric's body stiffened. "Someone got past security?"

"I was hoping it was one of you checking things out."

"We're good, Drake, but not that good. Maybe Ramsey could do it, but not me. And not Carey Johnson. He was the one assigned to you last night. You're sure it wasn't Trent?"

"No. I'm not sure."

"Anything missing?"

Xavier decided not to mention the ring. "Ask Trent when you find him. I'm assuming he's still missing?"

"As far as I know he is." Holmes suddenly swore, looking past him. Xavier pivoted as Holmes went for his weapon. A man was attempting to pull Zoe from the car. Xavier began to run.

"Police!" A woman's voice shouted from somewhere. "Drop your gun!"

Xavier didn't search for the source of the voice. He barely noted the gun in the man's hand as he ran at him. "Let her go!"

Instead the man pulled a struggling Zoe against his chest. She kicked back hard at his shin and let herself go limp. Her attacker wasn't prepared for the sudden deadweight in his arms. He released her before she pulled him down and brought his gun up on Xavier.

Xavier felt the wind's passage as the bullet sailed past his cheek. The morning was suddenly peppered with gunfire.

The man swung toward the house and the source of the other shots as Xavier continued toward Zoe. She'd scooted back against the car's wheel.

The gunman suddenly crumpled in front of her, red spouting from his neck and chest. Xavier reached for her and Zoe buried her face in his chest.

"Nice kick."

She raised her face to his. "I never saw him until he opened the door."

"You did good."

"Is he dead?"

He held her face when she would have turned it toward the man on the ground. The man wasn't moving. "I don't know. Let's get you back in the car. We don't know where his brother is."

Holmes ran up as did a plainclotheswoman Xavier had never seen before. She was calling for backup, a gun clenched in her hand, her features grim as she checked the gunman and removed his weapon from his unresisting fingers.

"Are you okay?" she asked, turning to them.

"Yes, but there should be two of them."

"I know. Get her down in the car."

Xavier didn't waste his breath telling her that was what he was trying to do. Zoe cooperated and climbed into the backseat.

"Where did he come from?" Xavier demanded.

"I don't know."

Xavier pulled out his cell phone and dialed Sandy's number. Her voice was shrill and shaken when she answered.

"Are you and April okay?"

"Yes. Officer Cooper told us to go upstairs in the bedroom and stay there until she called us. Xavier, what's going on?"

"Your Officer Cooper shot one of the kidnappers. The other one is probably nearby. Where's April?"

"With me. Xavier, we're scared. We need you."

"Go," Zoe told him. Obviously she'd heard Sandy's plea. "I'll be fine. You need to protect April."

Sandy was squawking in his ear. He gazed at Zoe. "I love you."

Her lips parted in shock. "What did you say?"

Xavier shook his head. He hadn't meant to say it out loud. "Stay down." To Sandy he said, "I'm coming inside. Stay where you are."

He clicked shut the cell phone. Zoe was still staring at him with a stunned expression. "Holmes! We need to cover April and Sandy." To the detective he said, "I'm going inside to wait with Sandy and April. Don't let anyone near this car!"

The woman nodded and they raced across the lawn and into the house. People were peering out windows. Somewhere a dog barked. In the distance, sirens began to wail.

Xavier hit the front door running. "Cover the downstairs!"

He plunged up the stairs and ran to the master bedroom. The doors were closed. "Sandy?"

The door was flung wide. "Uncle Xavier!"

He swept April up, holding her tight. "You okay?" he asked Sandy over her shoulder.

"Yes! What's going on?"

"Is he dead?" April asked.

Xavier realized the bedroom window overlooked the front yard. "I don't know, baby."

"I hope it was the mean one."

He squeezed her and stood. "We've got a man downstairs, but just in case, I want you both to go inside the closet."

"Why?" Sandy demanded.

"As a precaution. We don't know where the other man is. I'll stay right here. No one is getting near either of you."

Reluctantly, Sandy ushered April into the walk-in closet as Eric Holmes called up to him. "Drake? It's clear down here."

"Come on up. I have Sandy and April isolated, but I haven't checked the rest of the place."

Holmes took the stairs in twos. "More cops are pulling up out front."

"Good."

"I'll check the other rooms."

Minutes later, the police took over. An ambulance arrived for the critically injured man, who turned out to be the nice one after all. Simon Schlosky was taken immediately into surgery. It was hours later before they learned that the police had executed a search warrant on Ike Schlosky's apartment and found that the man had hastily packed and fled.

Bloodstained clothing and towels led the police to believe he was injured, possibly shot at the park the night before. The police expected to pick him up quickly and Xavier realized his role was over. The police would take over the investigation. Schlosky would be too busy evading capture to come after anyone now so the threat to Zoe had just diminished.

There were still a lot of unanswered questions, however, including Harrison Trent's mysterious disappearance, but no doubt the police would find those answers once they talked with Simon Schlosky. Zoe didn't need to come with him to Florida any longer. He'd have no reason to see her again.

Except for the baby. Like April, the child would still be his niece or nephew. He could and would demand visitation rights, but that wasn't the same thing.

As what?

The question jolted him. What was it he thought would happen if she came with him? Did he think she'd give up her BMW and a penthouse suite to live with a man who made his living taking tourists out on the water?

Xavier knew better. He'd always known better. Zoe's life

was so far removed from his normal existence that he couldn't see a place where they could intersect beyond the baby. And he couldn't believe how much the thought hurt.

"Hey, you okay?"

Zoe touched his arm. He pulled back. She regarded him with puzzled eyes. Sitting there in Sandy's kitchen, they were surrounded by people, but for the moment, no one was paying the two of them any attention.

"I'm fine."

"You don't look fine."

"What do you want me to say?" *Forget about Trent? Come live with me? We'll be poor, but I'll make you happy? Yeah, right.* He'd give that relationship a month at most. Once the novelty wore off she'd be gone, just like Kath.

"It's over." His tone was bleak.

Her frown deepened. "They still have to find Harrison and the briefcase."

Xavier shrugged. He didn't care about the briefcase. And he especially didn't care about Harrison Trent. But she did. He needed to get out of there before he made a complete fool of himself.

"I need to talk to the officer in charge," he told her, shoving back the chair and standing quickly, before he did or said something they would both regret. He felt her startled gaze following him across the room.

Zoe watched him go, her chest tight. Xavier should have been happy now that there was little threat to her or April.

The thought stopped her cold. He would go back to Florida and now there was no reason for her to go with him.

Except that she wanted to go.

Bleakly, she studied his features as he spoke with the detective. Xavier had said he loved her. But that had been in the heat of the moment. He hadn't repeated the words. He hadn't even touched her since the police had arrived. Was he regretting his words?

They'd gone from one stressful situation to another in a matter of days. Their attraction was combustible, but wasn't that the way it had been with his brother?

No. Flattery and sexual impulse had driven that short-lived relationship. She hadn't admired or respected Wayne. But how could she trust her feelings for Xavier in such a short period of time?

She was engaged. Harrison was still missing. There was something wrong with her if she could go from one man to another this way.

April joined Xavier when the detective turned away, and Xavier focused on his niece. Xavier loved his brother's child enough to risk everything for her. Who wouldn't be drawn to a man like that? She touched her stomach and blinked back tears.

Her baby wasn't a stumbling block, but Xavier barely knew her. She knew firsthand how easy it was to confuse attraction with love. But how could they know for sure if he left and she stayed here?

She didn't *need* Xavier. She had a job she was good at, a condo she still owned, and friends to support her emotionally. There was plenty of time to make life-altering decisions. Her baby had to come first now, and Zoe was perfectly capable of raising her child herself.

She would not marry Harrison. Her reaction to Xavier had shown her how wrong that marriage would be.

Sandy joined Xavier and April. Zoe shoved down the emotion welling in her chest as the three of them stood there talking, looking for all the world like a family unit. Drawing in a deep breath, she rose from her seat and crossed to them. She felt Sandy's animosity as the woman glared at the interruption.

"I'm sorry to intrude but I was wondering if the detective would let us go now."

"I was just telling Sandy I need to run you back to the penthouse."

"I don't want to take you away from your family. I'll ask Mr. Holmes for a ride."

His jaw tightened. "I'll take you."

"No." She held his gaze. "You should stay here. I'll send your suitcase back by courier."

Sandy covered his arm possessively. "April and I will feel much better if you'd stay here."

He held Zoe's gaze with troubled eyes. It should have been comforting to know that he was as conflicted as she was, but Zoe wasn't comforted in the least.

"If you're sure?"

She managed a smile. "I'm sure. It will be fine, Xavier."

XAVIER COULDN'T SEE HOW it would be fine at all.

He'd watched her leave with Eric Holmes and his gut had clenched. But when April had slid her hand trustingly into his, he had known there wasn't any choice. He and Sandy needed to make plans.

Now Xavier stood in the lobby of Harrison Trent's building and scowled darkly at the man behind the desk.

"I'm sorry, sir. Ms. Linden is not answering the telephone. If you'd like to leave a message—"

"I've already left a message."

The man shifted uncomfortably. Xavier tried to look less threatening. The man was only doing his job. And either Zoe had turned off her cell phone or she'd forgotten to charge her battery. His calls had gone straight to voice mail, which was no reason to panic, but worry gnawed at him. He didn't want to cause a scene that could turn ugly and embarrass her if there was no need and there was one person who might be able to reassure him. He walked away from the desk. Eric Holmes picked up on the second ring.

"It's Drake."

"Yeah. I saw you arrive."

"Is she okay?"

"She's fine."

"You're sure? She isn't answering her phone."

"Maybe she doesn't want to talk to you."

He ignored that. "I'm taking April to Florida with me tonight. I want Zoe to come until this is cleared up."

Holmes sighed. "I knew you were going to let it get messy."

He ignored that. "Your people haven't found Trent yet?"

"We're working on it."

"Maybe she isn't as safe as we might think."

"That hasn't escaped our attention, Drake. Trent's going to have a hefty fee when he puts in an appearance again." The man sighed once more.

"So if she doesn't want to come with us you'll stick to her?"

"Like glue."

"Ask her to call me, will you?"

Holmes hesitated. "All right."

"Thanks. If you ever get to Florida, look me up. I'll take you sailing, deep-sea fishing, if you like to fish."

There was a trace of surprise in his tone. "I might take you up on that one day."

"Do it."

"Take care of yourself and the kid."

"Always." Xavier disconnected. The rest was up to Zoe. He'd scared her off, saying *I love you* the way he had. She was engaged and pregnant. They barely knew each other. He'd been a fool.

He stood beside the rental car in the fire lane and debated

his options. As he did, a dark-blue BMW pulled out of the underground parking lot. The driver was too far away to see clearly, but he knew it was her. He jumped in the car and gave chase. She didn't go far or he might have lost her in the bustle of late-morning traffic. She pulled into a busy strip mall shopping center and parked in front of a pharmacy. While she lucked into a spot right in front of the store, he had to circle to find a place to park.

She'd already gone inside by the time Xavier reached her car. The backseat was filled with boxes and clothing. His heart began pounding. He recognized the briefcase. She was moving out of the penthouse? No wonder she hadn't answered.

A silent part of him cheered. She wasn't going to wait for Trent. But the rational part of him wanted to shake her. Didn't she realize she was still at risk until the police picked up the other Schlosky brother?

A large supermarket delivery truck executed the tight turn into the shopping center. It blocked several cars as the driver tried to maneuver into the alley behind the store. Xavier looked away as Zoe exited the pharmacy like a woman on a mission. She stopped dead the moment she saw him. "Xavier?"

He couldn't say what alerted him. Maybe the whine of the car engine or a reflection in the glass storefront. Something sent him lunging for her, fear in every fiber of his being.

Her eyes widened in shock as he jerked her back against the plate-glass window. Shots spattered the area. Someone screamed, loudly and shrilly. The window at Zoe's back sprang multiple holes.

Xavier heard tires squealing as he pulled her down to the sidewalk and covered her with his body. It was over in an instant. Then there was chaos.

Chapter Twelve

"Are you all right?" Xavier demanded.

Shaken, Zoe nodded. "I think so."

"Keep down. The car could come back for another pass." He didn't think it likely, but the shooter must be desperate to make another attempt at her in broad daylight in a crowded spot like this one.

He pulled out his cell phone and dialed 911. "Police emergency. There's been a shooting. We need police and ambulances at…" He looked around for a sign. Zoe gave him the name of the shopping center. He repeated it into the phone even as he moved beside the man who'd exited the store behind Zoe. Bright red blood stained the side of his shirt.

"I've been shot!" he kept repeating.

"An ambulance is on the way," Zoe told him.

Xavier bent and looked at his wound. "You're okay. The bullet passed straight through. You're going to be fine." He pulled off his shirt and wadded it up, pressing against the wound in the man's side. "Hold this right here. You're going to be okay."

The man nodded. Someone else was sobbing. He twisted to see Zoe talking to a woman clutching a toddler to her chest.

"You're scaring your daughter. Let me have a look. We need to be sure she's okay."

The woman finally let Zoe take the child, who was crying uncontrollably in fear. People were gathering around, exclaiming loudly. Xavier didn't see blood on the child or the mother.

Eric Holmes ran up. "How bad are you hurt?"

"We've got a man down over there."

A woman was tending to the injured man, pressing against the shirt Xavier had given him. "And this lady and her child had a bad scare, but it looks like everyone else is okay."

"You're bleeding, Drake."

Zoe inhaled sharply. For the first time Xavier realized blood ran down his bare arm from a hole several inches below the tape from the last wound.

"You've got to be kidding me. It's the same damn arm."

"Good thing you're right-handed." Zoe tried out a wobbly smile as she took his good arm and tried to pull him down. "Sit down before you fall down."

"I'm not going to fall." But abruptly the arm began to hurt.

"Sit down, hero."

Xavier let Zoe draw him down to the sidewalk. "Holmes, was it Schlosky?"

The other man's expression was sheepish. "I don't know. My car was blocked by that delivery truck. I didn't realize what was happening until I heard the shots. By the time I got here, the car was speeding away. I didn't get a clear look. Let's hope someone else did."

Xavier swore. Zoe was still holding his good arm. He clutched her hand. "Bathing suit or no bathing suit, you're coming to Florida with me."

"How soon can we leave?"

HIS SISTER MET THEM at the airport along with half the younger members of the family. April greeted her cousins enthusiastically and began chattering away. Xavier felt as if every nerve ending was stretched taut. His arm ached like the devil because he'd refused to take the prescription pain medication, taking two of Zoe's ibuprofen instead.

Lorraine eyed the sling on his left arm and narrowed her eyes. "What did you do?"

"He got shot," April piped up.

"Shot?"

"Xavier likes playing hero," Zoe told her. "He's actually quite good at it."

Lorraine's gaze landed on Zoe. "I take it you're Xavier's mystery pregnant woman?"

She slanted Xavier a look. "Mystery pregnant woman?"

Xavier raised his good palm in protest. "I didn't call you that."

"Where's Sandy and how bad is your arm?" Lorraine demanded of him.

"You know Sandy. She hates to fly. She's going to drive down in a few days. And it's just a scratch."

"The first one was a scratch," Zoe corrected him. "This one went clear through. He won't be rigging sails for a few days."

"You were shot *twice?*"

Lorraine's voice escalated, making Xavier acutely aware of all the interested ears. The children had fallen silent.

"In the same damn arm," April chimed in. At the instant scolding she shrugged. "Well, that's what you told Mom. The first time he was only greased."

"Creased," Zoe corrected. "That's like a scratch. The first time the bullet almost missed completely. The second time it didn't."

"Cool." Jimmy's bright eyes were wide with excitement. "What happened the third time?"

Feeling exasperated, Xavier glared at Zoe. "There was no third time."

"The gunman got away," April announced.

"How come you didn't catch him, Uncle Xavier?"

"Yeah," one of the others demanded.

"He was too busy rescuing April and me," Zoe told them.

"Who're you?" his nephew asked.

"I'm Zoe."

"Could we take this somewhere else?" Xavier demanded. A few people nearby had paused to listen.

"I agree." Lorraine took charge instantly. "Let's get your bags and head for the van. This is a story that is obviously going to require chocolate if not something stronger. Welcome to Florida, Zoe."

"Thank you. And thank you for inviting me to stay with you. I could go to a motel," Zoe told his sister.

"Only if you find the patter of my herd of elephants too obnoxious to bear. With three kids, my place tends to be on the noisy side."

"I like kids."

"You say that now. Wait until you get to know my little monsters." But her gaze was filled with love as she regarded the children plying April with questions while they waited for the luggage.

"I'm looking forward to it," Zoe assured her.

"Ha." Lorraine turned to Xavier. "I had to do some rearranging, but the *Mary Ellen* is coming in tonight. You can have it for the next five days. I know you wanted a week, but we're booked solid."

"Five days will be great."

"Maybe not. Tropical storm Finley is on the move and they've posted warnings all along the coastline. The water will be rough even though they don't expect it to turn inward. I'm not sure you can manage with just the kids, Xavier."

"Hey," Zoe protested, "I can crew. It's been a while, but I think with a quick refresher course I'll be fine to help out."

"We aren't going to head anywhere in particular," Xavier

told his sister. Lowering his voice, he added, "I want to get Zoe and April out on the water where it will be harder for anyone to get near them. I guess I need to explain the situation."

Lorraine nodded. "In detail. And you may as well start your rehearsal with me. You'll have to go over it all again at the inquisition tonight. Mom's making potato salad and cookies, Darlene's making her infamous chocolate cake and deviled eggs, Audra's doing dip and the fruit salad you like so much, and I'm bringing a vegetable bake and homemade rolls. The men are contributing the protein and drinks and Dad's firing up the grill." To Zoe she added, "My family doesn't do anything by half measures so if you don't want to gain a gazillion pounds tonight take small tastes of everything, and hide your plate."

"I'll bring the peanut butter," Xavier offered and was rewarded when Zoe blushed.

Lorraine scolded him with a glance and helped load suitcases on the cart she'd rented. "Peanut butter, huh? With my last one it was ice cream. You're—what—three months along?"

"Over four, actually."

"And still having morning sickness?"

"Not at all. I just don't take well to being tossed off a balcony, running from a pair of gunmen or being driven by a race car driver wannabe."

Zoe smiled sweetly over her shoulder at him and Xavier groaned.

"You dropped her off a balcony?"

"Sure, great. Gang up on me. I'm injured here, remember? We're on the ground three minutes and you've already joined forces with my sister."

Zoe arched her eyebrows and smiled sweetly. "I like your sister."

"Oh, she's going to fit right in," Lorraine promised.

"That's what I'm afraid of."

Zoe laughed and moved off with his sister, the two of them chatting like a pair of old friends. And Zoe did fit right in with his family. Xavier watched her closely when his family gathered in his parent's backyard for the impromptu family cookout. He was ready to come to her rescue, only to watch the women work and chat together like they'd been doing so all their lives. Zoe swept back her hair absently and laughed at something Darlene told her. His chest tightened. She was so lovely.

His brother-in-law put a cold beer in his good hand. "About time you found someone."

"Thanks, Bill. It isn't like that."

"Hey, buddy, I've been watching you watch her for the past ten minutes. It's exactly like that."

"She's engaged."

"Engaged isn't married. She's here with you, isn't she? I don't see her loving fiancé taking any bullets to protect her."

"I told you, we don't know what happened to him."

"Right."

"You going to marry the woman or what?" Audra's husband, Rory, asked, coming up beside them.

Xavier rolled his eyes and shook his head. "You, too? I'm going to go talk to Dad."

"Was it something I said?" Rory asked, grinning mischievously.

"You used the *M* word," Bill told him. "Sends a bachelor running every time."

Xavier ignored them and crossed to the grill, where his father labored over beef and seafood.

"How's the arm, son?" his father greeted him.

"Sore, if you want the truth."

"Got something to take for it?"

"Nothing I want to use."

His father nodded in understanding. "I remember what it's like. I took a bullet through the thigh in Vietnam. Scar aches to this day when it's cold and damp outside."

Xavier cocked his head. "I didn't know that."

"No reason you should. It was a long time ago. For what it's worth, son, I heartily approve." He nodded toward Zoe as he flipped a tuna steak.

Xavier groaned. "Not you, too."

"You were meant to be a family man. I'm glad to see your brother's taste improved even if his morals didn't."

That stopped him. "You know her baby is Wayne's?"

His father's head jerked up and Xavier realized his mistake.

"Not until now." He returned his attention to the hot grill while Xavier muttered a curse.

"Don't worry, I won't say anything. Is that part of your problem? She's having Wayne's baby?"

"No!" He inhaled deeply. "I don't have a problem."

But he caved under the penetrating look his father gave him. Even as a boy, he'd never been able to lie or keep a secret from his father.

"Okay, I have a problem, but it isn't because she's pregnant. I don't care whose baby it is. A child isn't its parent."

"True, but I thought maybe after what Wayne did to you with Kath—"

"Wayne did Kath and me both a favor in the long run. It took a while, but I finally recognized that. She wanted different things out of life than I do."

His father nodded in satisfaction. "And you think Zoe wants those things, too?" he asked shrewdly. "Hold that plate for me, will you?"

Xavier set down his beer and picked up the serving platter one-handed, stabilizing it with his sling arm. His father began transferring beautifully seared pieces of meat and fish from the grill.

"Zoe's a big-league VIP," Xavier told him. "She drives a BMW. She's engaged to a man who owns a penthouse that spans two floors on top of a huge building. That skirt she's wearing probably cost more than this grill."

"And you think money's that important to her?"

Did he? "Isn't it to most people?"

His father glanced from Zoe to him. "It is to some people but you've got five days to find out if it's true for Zoe and maybe show her different." He looked Xavier in the eye. "You're a thousand times the man your brother was, Xavier. Don't sell yourself short. Zoe strikes me as a very discerning person."

Touched by the words, Xavier sought something to say as his brother-in-law ambled over to join them. His father took the platter from him and handed it off to Rory. "Okay, everyone, food's ready."

ZOE ENDED UP AT the extended picnic table sitting across from and several people down from Xavier so she was free to watch him interact with his boisterous family. They were great. Zoe couldn't remember when she'd last laughed so much. The tension of the past few days melted away in this group.

As she studied the people around her, it was easy to see where Xavier and Wayne had gotten their good looks, and Wayne his generous measure of charm. Both parents were handsome, gracious, affable people who had welcomed her without a qualm.

Xavier took after his father while Wayne had looked more like his mother. Xavier's sisters were all extremely attractive and their families were exactly the way Zoe remembered her family being. Camaraderie and easy banter came from people who enjoyed each other's company and genuinely cared about each other despite any minor squabbles.

April had bloomed the moment she'd stepped off the plane. The trauma of the past week was bound to affect her, but it didn't show now. Zoe realized even she felt safe and at home in a way she hadn't since her family had died.

This was what she wanted for her child. And even if nothing came of her relationship with Xavier, Zoe's child would be a part of this wonderful family. And by extension, so would she. A comforting thought.

Xavier had also changed since they'd landed. The lines of tension and strain were fading from his features. He looked several years younger as he teased and was teased in return by his relatives. Uncle Xavier was an obvious favorite with all of the younger members.

She could love this man. Really love him. His caring, his sense of responsibility, his values, his…

"You going to make an honest man of my brother?"

Zoe turned to find Audra had plopped herself down in the seat beside her that Lorraine had just vacated. She could feel the heat rushing to her face.

"We've only shared a bed, not each other."

Audra shook her head. "What is wrong with you, woman? He may be my brother, but I know prime when I see it. Those dimples of his are real killers! Of course, the downside is that he does have to fight the women off with a baseball bat. Darlene and I could have made a fortune hiring him out for stud, you know."

Zoe sputtered a laugh.

"Hey, I'm serious here. We have girlfriends that have done everything but throw their naked bodies down in front of him. And come to think of it, Janine might have even gone that far. Wait until you see him with his shirt off."

"I have."

"I meant without blood flowing."

"Audra!"

"You won't meet a finer man," she added without humor.

All Zoe could do was nod mutely. "I'm engaged, Audra. Until we learn what happened to my fiancé…"

Audra waved that away with an impatient hand. "Engagements can be broken."

"Yes, they can. But if I've learned anything in the past five months, it's that I'm not rushing into another relationship." She patted her stomach. "I have a baby to consider now."

Audra settled back, oozing confidence. "That's okay. He'll wait."

"Audra!"

"Is my sister giving you a hard time?"

Xavier was suddenly towering over her and she had the worst feeling he'd overheard their last few comments.

"Come on. Let's walk off some of these calories we just consumed."

"I have to help clean up first."

Audra shook her head. "You helped set up. Besides, the women did most of the cooking so the men will clean up. That's the deal and that's why he wants you to walk with him."

"Brat." Xavier raised his sling. "I was given dispensation. Bill thinks I'll be more of hindrance than a help." He held out his other hand to Zoe. "What do you say?"

Aware of several sets of eyes watching the scene, Zoe hesitated. Then she placed her hand in his, swung her legs over the bench and let him help her up.

Sunset stained the sky with fading color as a soft breeze wafted up from the water only a few blocks away. All too aware of his large hand still clasping hers, she tugged free under the guise of smoothing her skirt.

Two of the older kids came running over. "Can we come, too, Uncle Xavier?"

"Sure, why not?"

At the same time Lorraine and Audra both said no.

"Mo-om," they cried in unison.

"They're fine. We're just going to walk down to the water so I can give Zoe a glimpse of the *Mary Ellen*."

Lorraine sighed. "Are you sure?"

"Can I come, too, Uncle Xavier?"

He ruffled April's hair. "Of course you can. The more the merrier."

The mothers drew the line at the younger Drakes tagging along, but even without them, Zoe felt a little like a mother duck as they herded five rambunctious children down the sidewalk of the small, middle-class development.

"How's the sales pitch going?" he asked.

"What?"

"My sisters. You aren't going to tell me they aren't trying to sell you on what a great husband I'd make."

Humor glinted in his eyes. Zoe raised her eyebrows. "The way I heard it, they make more money offering you out for stud duties."

His expression was priceless.

"They actually said that?"

"Words to that effect."

"I'll put frogs in their beds."

Zoe smiled. "Their husbands might object. Come to that, so might the frogs."

"There is that."

"Would you?" She regretted the question as soon as the words were spoken.

He cocked his head. "Make a good husband?"

Zoe looked toward the chattering children, hoping he wouldn't notice her disconcerted blush.

"I think so. One day. Don't let them harass you. They

mean well, but they've been trying to marry me off for years. They like you."

"I like them, too. Your entire family is great."

"Thank you. I agree."

They walked on in companionable silence while the children danced around them, chatting amiably. "Why was your brother—"

"A thief?"

"I was going to say so different, but essentially, yes."

"I don't know. My parents don't know. I could say Wayne was the baby and he was spoiled rotten, but the truth is, my parents didn't really spoil any of us." He scowled, looking straight ahead, but obviously seeing something from another time. "Wayne was always different. A baby wants what it wants when it wants it. But despite my parent's best efforts, Wayne never outgrew that mentality."

He paused, considering. "No, that isn't fair. It was more that Wayne viewed life as a gigantic game of one-upmanship, where the winner takes all. He used to lie straight-faced over nothing at all just for the fun of seeing who he could get to believe him."

"With all his charm, I'm sure he had no trouble convincing everyone."

Xavier sighed. "Too true. He hated the family lifestyle. It wasn't just what they did, as much as what my parents no longer did. Dad has an MBA and mom is a CPA. He felt they wasted their degrees running tourists out in the gulf."

"Because he didn't like boats."

"No, because *our* boats don't come with crews to do all the manual labor. Wayne didn't like work that wasn't of his choosing. He was fine with schmoozing the customers, but he didn't want to bait a hook, clean a galley, fix a meal, that sort of thing. Dad put us to work as soon as we were old enough to hold a mop." He slid a glance at her. "Ours is a pretty simple lifestyle, Zoe. As you see," he gestured toward the neighborhood, "we don't run to penthouses around here."

"Was that a dig, Xavier?"

"No." His jaw tightened. "I'm merely pointing out the differences between how we live and what Wayne wanted out of life."

"Uh-huh. And what do you want?"

He was saved from answering by two of the younger boys who demanded he arbitrate an argument. With gentle good humor, he did. They were still some distance from the water, but they had stopped at a spot where they could overlook the pier and the boats moored there.

"The one on the end there is the *Mary Ellen*," he told her.

"Big boat."

"Sleeps six," he agreed. "We have two that size that we rent out by the week or month. If things go well this year, we're hoping to add another one a bit larger. Sometimes we crew it, sometimes the renters just lease the boat."

"What's the significance of the name?"

"Mary Ellen was my grandmother on my father's side. The other boat is the *Nancy's Luck* after Mom's mother, but it's my dad's family that comes from a long line of fishermen."

"Are we going down to the boat, Uncle Xavier?"

"No, Brian, we're going to head back now."

"Can we stop at your house and play some video games?"

"Yeah, can we, Uncle Xavier?" piped in one of the girls. Zoe thought it was Amy but she looked so much like her cousin Christy it was hard to tell the two girls apart.

"Not tonight. I imagine Grandma has cake and cookies ready by now."

Zoe tipped her head to one side. "Your house is nearby?"

"Yes."

She sensed his unease, but April was already tugging on her hand. "Come on, I'll show you where it is. Mom and I always stay there when we come down together. Mom says it's too small, but I think it's perfect."

"It's cool," Brian enthused. "He has all kinds of movies and video games and a dartboard and big yard next door where we can play baseball and football and stuff."

Xavier looked uncomfortable as Zoe let April tug her down a side street. He caught up to them in a couple of steps.

"The house is pretty small," he warned.

"What would you need with a big house?" Zoe asked. "I don't imagine you're home much."

"No. Actually, I often sleep on the *Mary Ellen*. Since I'm single, I generally crew the long runs with one of the people who crew for us regularly. I enjoy the work."

"It's the next street," April piped up, dropping Zoe's hand and skipping ahead to be with her cousins.

"The house next to mine was destroyed in a fire a few years ago," Xavier explained. "The owners didn't want to rebuild so I bought the land and had it cleared to give the kids a place to play when they came over."

The ground-hugging house sat on a corner lot and did appear quite small from the outside. It also looked cozy and welcoming. The grounds were well maintained and had a surprising number of mature trees and land between the house and its nearest neighbor.

"I think it looks charming. It must be nice living so close to your parents."

Xavier shrugged, still looking uncomfortable. "It has its benefits. Mom likes to cook and I like to eat so I can pretty much cage a free meal whenever I want."

The kids had all moved on ahead of them, laughing and talking together in high spirits. Satisfied they were out of earshot, she slanted him a glance. "Why do I get the feeling your fiancée made you feel ashamed of your home?"

His steps faltered a second as they passed by the house. "Someone told you about Kath?"

"Only that you were engaged and Wayne broke you up."

His eyes narrowed. "It wasn't that simple."

"Things rarely are. You don't need to explain."

Xavier seemed to relax. "I don't mind. And for the record, I'm not ashamed of my house. It's a nice little place, but if we stop now I'll never get the kids back over to Mom's. Later on I'll give you the grand tour. It will take all of three minutes."

"I'd like that."

They continued to walk, following the children. "Kath was a long time ago," Xavier told her quietly. "Her dad worked with mine before we set up the family business. We'd known each other since grade school. I ran into her after I came out of the service and we started dating." He shrugged. "Our families were pleased and one thing led to another. We more or less fell into a relationship."

"Sounds like Harrison and me."

His gaze dropped to hers in question, but she waited him out without saying any more.

"Eventually, we set a wedding date, but as it grew closer I sensed Kath wasn't happy. I thought it was because I was making so many long runs on the *Mary Ellen*. Crewing like that pays well in tips and I was trying to set aside as much money as I could before the wedding. I had to come back early from one run when the weather turned nasty. I found Kath and Wayne in my bed."

"I'm sorry."

"So was I at the time." His shoulders rose and fell in dismissal. "In the end, though, it worked out for the best. Kath eventually married someone who moved her to New York and the sort of life she was meant to have."

Xavier was a little surprised at how easy it was to tell Zoe. He kept expecting a twinge of pain at the memory, but there wasn't any. Kath and his brother were part of the past and he was quite happy to leave them there.

"Very philosophical of you."

He tipped his head to one side. "What does that mean?"

"That I hope Harrison will be as understanding when I give him his ring back."

Xavier caught his breath. There was such certainty in her voice. His stomach twisted uncomfortably. "Because of a couple of kisses? I wouldn't be hasty, Zoe. You may change your mind."

"Think highly of yourself, don't you?"

He stopped walking. She stopped as well.

"You can take that stricken look right off your face, Xavier Drake. As much as I like you, I'm not dumping Harrison because you kissed me. Or even because you threw yourself in front of a couple of bullets for me. I'm returning his ring because we were about to make a gigantic mistake and in my heart I knew it before you ever climbed through my balcony door. I love Harrison. I will always love Harrison."

He couldn't breathe.

"I'm just not *in* love with Harrison. He's a great person. You'll like him. In fact, the two of you are a lot alike. We could have made our marriage work, but it would have been the wrong choice for both of us. I won't make that mistake again."

He searched her face, looking for answers to the questions running through his mind. Her expression was utterly serene.

"I'm not sure I understand."

"It doesn't matter. I understand, and I think Harrison will, too. You know I'm strongly attracted to you. I won't pretend

I'm not. And," she added with a small smile, "you do know how to kiss."

Some of his tension drained away. "But?"

"But I am not making any more long-term commitments."

He cocked his head. She appeared relaxed but determined. He let his lips curve just the slightest bit. "Ever?"

Immediately, humor danced in her eyes. "I should have said I'm not rushing into any more relationships."

"Okay. That's reasonable."

"I'm glad you think so."

Xavier took that as a positive sign.

"You're very sweet."

He grimaced. "Sweet."

"Sweet," she agreed with a soft smile.

"Like in saccharine?"

"As in someone I want to take my time and get to know better."

"I like the sound of that."

"So do I." Her sigh seemed to be directed inward. "Look, I know you've seen little evidence of it, but I *can* take care of myself. At least most of the time when I don't have people trying to kill me."

"Zoe, I don't doubt that for a moment. You strike me as a woman who can do anything you set your mind to."

The kids turned the corner onto his parents' street. "Come on before they miss us." He started walking again and she fell into step beside him.

Zoe wasn't telling him to get lost. She was asking for time. Xavier respected that. No matter how much he wanted her, he didn't want to make another mistake either. Despite her acceptance of his family and his home, he couldn't stop seeing her inside that penthouse and thinking it was right for her.

"I just wanted to be clear with you," Zoe continued, "so there are no misunderstandings."

"Fair enough. I'm not comfortable in the role of the other man here." He held up a hand when she would have interrupted. "We have very different lifestyles, Zoe, and I'm not going to pretend to be other than what I am. I like my life and I like my house." He smiled for a second and she acknowledged the words with an answering lift to her lips.

"I don't need or want a penthouse or a BMW or designer jeans. I don't know you well enough to know how important those things are to you, but it's something we both need to consider. I thought I knew Kath, but it turned out those things were very important to her. Like you, I don't want to make another mistake. But don't ask me to pretend I don't want you, because I do."

She stopped walking and her lips parted. Somehow, his hand came to rest on her shoulder. His body sang with need the moment he touched her. Her eyes darkened in response. She lifted her face.

"Uncle Xavier?"

He turned away as Amy came running back up to them.

"Mom says to tell you the cleanup's done and dessert's on the table and you'd better come now if you want any."

With a rueful smile, he released Zoe and ruffled Amy's hair. "Timing is everything."

"Yes," she breathed.

For a long moment they simply stared at one another.

"Are you coming?" Amy asked impatiently. "Aunt Lorraine made chocolate cake."

Zoe smiled at the child. "We can't let chocolate cake go to waste. Any chance there are peanut butter cookies to go with it?"

Chapter Thirteen

Tropical storm Finley veered away from the Florida coastline and spent herself out in the open waters as if tired of the entire process. Xavier took the extra day to lay in provisions and clean the *Mary Ellen* while Zoe familiarized herself with its operations. She had only been exposed to much smaller pleasure boats.

The three oldest children worked diligently without complaint until the boat sparkled inside and out.

"Come on. Ice cream's on me," Xavier announced.

Zoe looked up from the seat where she'd plopped down in the late-afternoon sun and gazed up at him. "Does it require moving?"

"Tired?"

"Whatever gave you that impression?"

His dimples flashed, sending a pang of longing zipping through her. It wasn't fair. His smile should be registered as a lethal weapon.

"Okay, you earned your keep today. I guess I could go and bring you back something."

"Maybe they have peanut butter ice cream," April suggested with a naughty grin.

Zoe wagged a finger at the girl. "That's a low blow, kiddo. But if they do, I'll take a small dish."

Xavier laughed. "How about an ice-cream sundae with peanuts on top?"

"Mmm. I could handle that, too."

"Okay. You rest while we take a walk down the boardwalk."

He bent and kissed the top of her hair as if it was the most natural thing in the world to do, a loving mark of possession. Warmth filled her. How many times had she seen her father do that with her mother?

"I'll be back in a few minutes. Don't fall asleep out here without putting on more sunscreen."

How could she not love him? "Yes, bossy."

"It's aye, aye, Captain."

She stuck out her tongue at him. The children laughed.

"Come on, gang. Let's let Zoe take a nap or she might get cranky on us."

"Cranky?" she demanded indignantly.

Xavier winked. "We'll be right back."

Zoe closed her eyes, smiling. The sun's warm rays baked her skin with delicious warmth. A light breeze drifted across the water, making for a wonderful sensation. She could get used to this.

After several minutes she roused herself enough to think about moving inside, but couldn't bring herself to open her eyes. She was tired, but it was a good sort of tired. The baby stirred inside her and she rubbed her stomach lightly.

She was more asleep than awake when someone stepped aboard. Zoe blinked up at the figure sleepily. The sun was in her eyes so all she saw was the outline at first.

"You're early."

Then she realized it wasn't Lorraine or Audra come to take her shopping.

"Sandy?" Wide-awake, she straightened up, blood drumming in her ears.

"Where's Xavier?"

Cold alarm slammed through Zoe. While Zoe understood the woman's resentment, there was something almost menacing in the way Sandy towered over her, gripping the large purse hanging from one shoulder.

"Xavier went for ice cream. He should be back any second now," she lied, scrambling to her feet.

"Is April with him?"

"Yes." Zoe strove to sound calm and unalarmed while her body hummed with nervous tension. "We weren't expecting you yet, but April will be happy to see you."

"I found the briefcase."

For a moment, Zoe couldn't make sense of the non sequitur. "You mean the briefcase the Schloskys were looking for?"

Sandy's head jerked in a nod. "It was in the trunk of my car. We need to find Xavier."

"Did you call the police?"

"I didn't find it until today when I went looking for the spare tire," she snapped. "I got a flat on my way here."

The banked rage in her eyes was all wrong. Fear set up a strident clanging in Zoe's head. She looked down the dock for any sign of rescue.

"I think I was followed here."

"Oh."

Sandy had good reason to be agitated if that was the case. There was still one Schlosky brother unaccounted for.

"I need Xavier."

Zoe stepped into the deck shoes she'd toed off while she was lying there. "They just walked down the boardwalk. Let me get my cell phone. We'll call him."

"We need to leave now! We're too exposed." Sandy looked back over her shoulder. "We could be trapped here."

If Sandy had been followed, this could prove a dead end for both of them.

"There are thousands of dollars worth of gems in the trunk of my car. Don't you understand the danger?"

Her stomach twisted. "Sandy, calm down."

The other woman fingered her shoulder bag. Her eyes burned with fear, anger and resentment. "I don't want to calm down! I want Xavier!"

"All right." Sandy was freaking her out. Getting off the boat suddenly did seem like a good idea. "Let's go."

Instead of turning, Sandy stepped aside, waiting for Zoe to take the lead. Zoe's scalp prickled. She couldn't have said why, but she didn't want the other woman at her back.

"Come on," Sandy snarled.

Zoe's instincts screamed at her to run. Except there was nowhere to run to other than the direction they were heading. She should have gone inside the cabin and grabbed her cell phone and something to use as a weapon.

Why was she so afraid of Sandy?

Because it felt all wrong. Logic kicked in, reminding her that Sandy should be in Virginia, not here in Florida. She hated to fly and had claimed she needed a day or so to close up the house and cancel some appointments. She'd said she wouldn't join them for several days. But for her to be here now, she would have had to have left shortly after they had.

"I thought you weren't coming for a few days."

"I changed my mind, all right? I was worried about April."

Was Zoe reading the situation all wrong? Sandy might not like her, but she did seem to love her daughter.

As Zoe stepped off the boat she turned to look at her agitated companion. Sandy's expression was tight with malice and determination. Her hand had moved inside her shoulder bag.

Zoe's breath caught in her chest. There were people around, but no one close by. Deliberately, she stumbled and went down as they reached the end of the dock.

"Get up! We aren't safe yet!"

She shook her head. "I twisted my ankle."

Sandy swore. She removed her hand from her open bag. A short distance away a man started in their direction.

"Get up!"

Sandy bent to tug on her arm. Zoe used the woman's forward momentum to yank her off her feet. The shoulder bag spilled its contents over the ground and a revolver bounced and skittered several feet away. Zoe leaped up and began running as Sandy cursed.

XAVIER SPOTTED HIS brother-in-law walking toward them as they neared the ice-cream parlor. "Hey, Rory! I thought you had a charter this afternoon."

"I did. The group caught a couple of fish, but the water was so choppy, two of them got sick. They asked to come in early. Where are you headed?"

"Ice cream," Brian announced.

Rory grinned. "Sounds good. Mind if I join you?"

"Not at all."

"Where's Zoe?"

"Catching a nap on the deck."

Rory frowned and lowered his voice. "I thought Sandy was staying in Virginia for a few days."

Xavier tensed. "That's what she said, why?"

"I talked to Audra a few minutes ago. She was on her way back to the house to pick up Lorraine and said she saw Sandy pass her."

A deep sense of foreboding gripped Xavier. If Sandy was here now, something was wrong. He stopped walking. Pulling out his wallet, he handed Rory several bills. "Take the kids, will you? I need to get back to the *Mary Ellen*."

Rory's expression tightened in concern. "Something wrong?"

"That's what I'm going to find out. Keep a close eye on April."

"I'll take them back to Mom's when we're finished."

"Thanks." Xavier was already turning, loping back the way they had come. His sling slammed against his chest. He should never have left Zoe there alone and undefended. The two of them could be in danger.

Xavier ran faster.

ZOE HEARD SANDY pounding after her. She reached the parking lot and dodged between two parked SUVs. Her breathing came in short, hard pants as fear threatened to overwhelm her. Any second now she expected the sound of a gunshot. Instead, Sandy slammed into her back, spinning her around so hard she rammed into the nearest SUV, knocking the wind from her lungs.

"You stupid, crazy bitch! Do you want to get us killed?" Sandy shoved the gun against Zoe's throat. "I ought to shoot you right here and now."

"I'll do the shooting."

The man's raspy growl froze them both. Ike Schlosky stood behind Sandy, clenching a semiautomatic. The weapon was pointed right at them.

Sandy whirled. Her features were a mask of rage and fear. Before Zoe could draw a breath, Schlosky fired point-blank. The scream froze in Zoe's throat as Sandy collapsed on the ground. Sheer terror held her riveted in place.

"Where's the briefcase?"

There was steely determination in his eyes. Zoe began to shake. Her teeth actually chattered together.

"Sh…she said it was in the trunk of her car."

"Get her keys."

Zoe couldn't move.

"Get her keys now, bitch!"

Zoe looked down at the still form lying in a spreading pool of blood. For a moment, she thought she'd vomit. The baby moved as if her fear had communicated itself and Zoe bent with new determination. She would not let this man kill her or her baby. Whatever it took, she would do it.

XAVIER HEARD THE SHOT. He stopped, surveying the scene. Other people had paused to look around as well, but there was no obvious sign of trouble.

A minute later Zoe emerged from between a pair of hulking SUVs. A man walked at her side—so close they could have been taken as lovers. Except for Zoe's expression.

Xavier had to look hard to spot the gun in Schlosky's hand. He was marching her through the parking lot. Xavier couldn't let him put her in a car.

He bent quickly as if to tie his shoe as Schlosky swept the area with a tight gaze. Tension hummed through Xavier. He attempted to appear harmless and unconcerned. Zoe's life depended on his reactions.

The minute they passed, he stood. Zoe had looked right at him and never so much as twitched, but she'd seen and recognized him. He knew she had. He paralleled their course until they halted at a dark sedan with Virginia tags. Xavier lengthened his stride to close the distance between them. He prepared to launch himself at the man as Zoe unlocked the car trunk.

"Get the briefcase," Schlosky snarled.

Zoe obediently began to rummage inside the car trunk, pulling out a thick leather briefcase.

"Open it."

She set the case on the ground and did as instructed. Schlosky muttered something too low to hear and ordered her to step back. He crouched down over the case. Zoe took several quick steps back. The man fumbled to open a pouch inside the case.

Xavier knew this was the best chance he was going to get. He ran at the other man. Schlosky heard him and turned, bringing the gun up. Xavier hit him hard before he could fire, sending shiny bits of stones scattering.

He barely felt the pain in his arm as they struggled, intent on gaining control of the weapon. The sling reduced his mobility and Schlosky was fast. Xavier realized he wasn't going to win this one.

Schlosky suddenly pitched to one side.

Zoe hit him a second time with one of the large white, decorative rocks the marina used in their landscaping. She was bringing it down a third time when Eric Holmes appeared and lifted the rock from her hand.

"I've got it, Zoe."

Schlosky folded on the blacktop. Xavier snatched the gun from his hand and Zoe wrapped her arms around Xavier's neck. He winced, even as he drew her shaking body in close.

"Thanks," he whispered against her face.

"It was my turn." Her smile was shaky. Shock filled her eyes. "He shot Sandy."

Xavier looked at Eric Holmes. "What are you doing here?"

"I followed Sandy." He inclined his head toward Zoe. "One of the two of them had to have that briefcase and my money was on her. She's still alive, but…" He shook his head, indicating it was only a matter of time. "I called it in when I heard the shot. An ambulance and the police are on the way. I'm sorry. I lost her in town. By the time I spotted her car parked here, I was too far away when it went down."

"Where is she?"

"I'll show you." Zoe stood and helped him up, leading the way.

Xavier knelt beside Sandy, ignoring the pooling blood. One look and he knew Holmes was right. She was alive, but she wasn't going to make it without a miracle.

"Hang on, Sandy."

ZOE SQUEEZED HIS HAND when the doctor told them Sandy had died on the operating table. Xavier stared at Zoe bleakly. "I'd never cared for Sandy, but she was April's mother. How am I going to tell her both her parents are gone now?"

"You don't need to tell her everything. Keep it simple. You can tell her that Sandy died trying to get us both out of danger. April doesn't need to know anything else right now. Her mother drove down here because she was afraid of flying. When she changed her tire, she found the briefcase and realized she was being followed. She tried to warn us, but Schlosky appeared and killed her to get the briefcase. Wayne must have hidden it from his partners."

His troubled eyes pierced her with their intensity. "I love you."

"You say that now—"

"I'll say it when you're ready to listen as well." He drew her against his body, kissing her with enough tenderness to break her heart. He let her go and stepped back. "Thank you."

Zoe stared after him, longing to tell him she was ready to listen right now. But this wasn't the time or the place and she wasn't free to say what was in her heart. She turned away to find Eric Holmes watching.

"He's a good man."

Zoe could only nod.

"You okay?"

"No, but I will be, thanks to you. Did you really think one of us had the briefcase?"

"It seemed likely."

"Good thing she found it when she changed the tire."

He shook his head. "She never changed any tire."

"You're saying she had the briefcase all along?"

"Yes. Simon Schlosky is talking now that he's out of intensive care. Sandy was the second person in the gem heist. She's the one who shot the courier in cold blood."

Zoe winced, but she didn't doubt him.

"You know, Sandy's death was probably for the best. If she'd lived to stand trial, her little girl would have been caught up in a media frenzy that would have haunted her for the rest of her life. With any luck, this will fade away and she'll never learn the truth."

Zoe nodded. "At least not until she's old enough to understand. Her mother did love her."

He shrugged. "She was certainly possessive of whatever she saw as hers. A friend of hers claims Sandy was desperate to get Wayne Drake back. She went nuts when she found out he was dating you. She began putting pressure on Drake to come back to her or pay through the nose."

"She's the one who tried to kill me."

"Several times," Holmes agreed.

Zoe didn't know how to react. She'd suspected, but this was the first time anyone had said it out loud. "And the Schlosky brothers?"

"Simon Schlosky needed money to get his wife to come back to him. Turns out his next-door neighbor was the courier's brother. The men had drinks together one night and Simon pumped him for information. Then he called his brother. Ike has a police record and knew Wayne Drake from his jail time. The Schlosky brothers are a bit slow, but smart enough to take the information to Wayne who, I'm guessing, saw it as a way to get Sandy off his back."

"What a mess."

"Yeah. We'll never know why Sandy shot the courier, but you'll recall even Xavier said his brother would have gone ballistic over the murder. We're guessing Wayne left Sandy with the briefcase and washed his hands of the whole affair. He probably called you and proposed in an effort to get some other plan of his back on track."

"But he knew I was already engaged to Harrison."

"But you'd dumped him. From everything we've learned, that was a novel experience for him. He probably took it as a challenge to get you back."

"Gee, thanks." But she had a feeling Eric Holmes was probably right. "I only went to meet him that night to tell him about the baby. I thought he had a right to know."

And he'd sprung the proposal on her, refusing to take the ring back and pleading with her to think it over. Then suddenly he was dead without ever knowing about his child.

"We think Sandy was stalking Wayne," Eric continued. "And when she saw the two of you together again, she snapped."

"Was she trying to kill Wayne that night, or me?"

"I don't imagine she cared. Everyone says she had a temper. I think she opened fire out of spite. You survived, Wayne didn't. In her twisted way, she blamed you for his death."

Zoe tried to assimilate that. "If that's true, she could have traded the briefcase for April from the start."

"Not really. She didn't know Wayne's partners. They might not have let April go. Instead, she sent them after you. Remember, the police were already questioning her about Drake's death when Xavier showed up. She was sitting on over two million dollars in gems with Drake's partners are coming after her. And then there's you, the person she sees as the source of all her problems. If she can eliminate you and Drake's partners, she can take her daughter and the gems and disappear. That's the real reason she didn't fly down here with you and Xavier. She wanted to pack and clean out her bank accounts. I think she planned to kill you, grab her daughter and go."

"She shot Xavier twice!"

"Collateral damage. He wouldn't have been hurt if he hadn't tried to protect you." Eric shrugged.

"How can you know all this?"

"I don't for certain. At this point I'm mostly surmising, but getting inside a person's head is part of my job and I've been focusing on Sandy since I met you."

"I thought you were a bodyguard."

His smile was rueful. "That, too, but once Ramsey started looking into this thing, he discovered the insurance company is offering a huge reward. I thought it was worth a bit more digging and he gave me the okay. You're going to add a nice chunk of change to your bank account."

"Me? I had nothing to do with the briefcase's recovery. Innocent victim here, remember? You're the one who did all the work. I was just trying to stay alive."

He smiled. "Well, I think Ramsey will agree we should put some of the reward in trust for April. She may need it down the road."

"You're a good man, too, Eric Holmes. Thank you."

"Just invite me to the wedding, okay?"

XAVIER WATCHED APRIL and Lorraine's daughter Amy playing a video game together in his living room. April was subdued, but not withdrawn. Xavier had promised her she could live with him forever. Now he hoped he could keep that promise.

"She's doing well."

He turned to regard Zoe. "Better than I would have expected. Audra has a friend who's a counselor. She's already helped enormously. I'm going to apply to formally adopt April when things settle down."

"That's wonderful. She adores you, Xavier."

"And I love her. I always have."

"I know." She held his gaze. "How are you holding up?"

"Okay. Lorraine said you're making noises about going back to Virginia."

Her eyes darkened. "Eventually, I'll have to."

"I promised myself I wouldn't argue."

"Then keep that promise."

Hope plunged. He looked back at April. "I'm taking on a huge responsibility here."

She patted her stomach. "So am I."

"I want you to know you're family, Zoe. I'll always be here for you and your baby."

"Of course you will. You're her uncle."

He held her gaze. "I'd like to be more."

"I know. I think I'd like that, too."

His breath caught in his throat. "But?"

"I don't want to make another mistake."

"A long-distance relationship will make it tough to decide, don't you think? I have April to consider. I can't drop my life and fly to Virginia every weekend."

"I wouldn't ask you to. Lorraine has a friend who is looking for a house sitter for a year. I was thinking I might take her up on it. After all, I'm kind of used to having a bodyguard. You wouldn't be much use to me if I lived there and you lived here."

A weight seemed to lift from his chest. "What about your job?" What about Trent, he wanted to add.

Her eyes clouded. "When Harrison resurfaces, I'll take a

leave of absence. We already planned on that so it shouldn't be a problem."

"You think he'll simply go along with this?"

"Whatever is going on with him, he's my friend, Xavier. When the two of you meet you'll understand."

Xavier doubted it. "I wouldn't go along in his shoes."

She smiled then. "That's why I love you."

His heart stilled and then began to race. "You love me?"

"Hard not to. You have your full share of that Drake charm, you know."

"Zoe—"

She pressed a finger to his lips. "There's no comparison, Xavier. I know exactly who you are. I like who you are a great deal."

He captured her lips, fitting her body to his. Her arms circled his neck. She was leaning into him when the doorbell rang. He swore silently and released her. "Don't go anywhere."

"Wasn't planning to move."

"Good."

He threw open the door. Darleen's oldest boy stood there looking winded.

"Uncle Xavier, Dad said you should come down to the *Mary Ellen* right away. There's a man looking for Ms. Linden. His name is Harrison Trent."

Xavier turned to Zoe. The love in her steady gaze melted the sudden chill that had gripped him. She came forward and slid an arm around his waist.

"Good," she told the boy, her gaze returning to his. "I have a lot of explaining to do. And someone I want him to meet."

* * * * *

Zoe and Xavier have their happy future to plan,
but what did happen to the
mysterious Harrison Trent?
Don't miss Dani Sinclair's next
thrillingly romantic story,
THE MISSING MILLIONAIRE.
Available December 2008
only from Harlequin Intrigue!

Turn the page for a sneak preview of
AFTERSHOCK,
a new anthology
featuring New York Times
bestselling author
Sharon Sala.

Available October 2008.

n⬤cturne™

Dramatic and sensual tales
of paranormal romance.

Chapter 1

October
New York City

Nicole Masters was sitting cross-legged on her sofa while a cold autumn rain peppered the windows of her fourth-floor apartment. She was poking at the ice cream in her bowl and trying not to be in a mood.

Six weeks ago, a simple trip to her neighborhood pharmacy had turned into a nightmare. She'd walked into the middle of a robbery. She never even saw the man who shot her in the head and left her for dead. She'd survived, but some of her senses had not. She was dealing with short-term memory loss and a tendency to stagger. Even though she'd been told the problems were most likely temporary, she waged a daily battle with depression.

Her parents had been killed in a car wreck when she was twenty-one. And except for a few friends—and most recently her boyfriend, Dominic Tucci, who lived in the apartment right above hers—she was alone. Her doctor kept reminding her that she should be grateful to be alive, and on one level she knew he was right. But he wasn't living in her shoes.

If she'd been anywhere else but at that pharmacy when the

robbery happened, she wouldn't have died twice on the way to the hospital. Instead of being grateful that she'd survived, she couldn't stop thinking of what she'd lost.

But that wasn't the end of her troubles. On top of everything else, something strange was happening inside her head. She'd begun to hear odd things: sounds, not voices—at least, she didn't think it was voices. It was more like the distant noise of rapids—a rush of wind and water inside her head that, when it came, blocked out everything around her. It didn't happen often, but when it did, it was frightening, and it was driving her crazy.

The blank moments, which is what she called them, even had a rhythm. First there came that sound, then a cold sweat, then panic with no reason. Part of her feared it was the beginning of an emotional breakdown. And part of her feared it wasn't—that it was going to turn out to be a permanent souvenir of her resurrection.

Frustrated with herself and the situation as it stood, she upped the sound on the TV remote. But instead of *Wheel of Fortune,* an announcer broke in with a special bulletin.

"This just in. Police are on the scene of a kidnapping that occurred only hours ago at The Dakota. Molly Dane, the six-year-old daughter of one of Hollywood's blockbuster stars, Lyla Dane, was taken by force from the family apartment. At this time they have yet to receive a ransom demand. The housekeeper was seriously injured during the abduction, and is, at the present time, in surgery. Police are hoping to be able to talk to her once she regains consciousness. In the meantime, we are going now to a press conference with Lyla Dane."

Horrified, Nicole stilled as the cameras went live to where the actress was speaking before a bank of microphones. The shock and terror in Lyla Dane's voice were physically painful to watch. But even though Nicole kept upping the volume, the sound continued to fade.

Just when she was beginning to think something was wrong with her set, the broadcast suddenly switched from the Dane press conference to what appeared to be footage of the kidnapping, beginning with footage from inside the apartment.

When the front door suddenly flew back against the wall and four men rushed in, Nicole gasped. Horrified, she quickly realized that this must have been caught on a security camera inside the Dane apartment.

As Nicole continued to watch, a small Asian woman, who she guessed was the maid, rushed forward in an effort to keep them out. When one of the men hit her in the face with his gun, Nicole moaned. The violence was too reminiscent of what she'd lived through. Sick to her stomach, she fisted her hands against her belly, wishing it was over, but unable to tear her gaze away.

When the maid dropped to the carpet, the same man followed with a vicious kick to the little woman's midsection that lifted her off the floor.

"Oh, my God," Nicole said. When blood began to pool beneath the maid's head, she started to cry.

As the tape played on, the four men split up in different directions. The camera caught one running down a long marble hallway, then disappearing into a room. Moments later he reappeared, carrying a little girl, who Nicole assumed was Molly Dane. The child was wearing a pair of red pants and a white turtleneck sweater, and her hair was partially blocking her abductor's face as he carried her down the hall. She was kicking and screaming in his arms, and when he slapped her, it elicited an agonized scream that brought the other three running. Nicole watched in horror as one of them ran up and put his hand over Molly's face. Seconds later, she went limp.

One moment they were in the foyer, then they were gone.

Nicole jumped to her feet, then staggered drunkenly. The bowl of ice cream she'd absentmindedly placed in her lap shattered at her feet, splattering glass and melting ice cream everywhere.

The picture on the screen abruptly switched from the kidnapping to what Nicole assumed was a rerun of Lyla Dane's plea for her daughter's safe return, but she was numb.

Before she could think what to do next, the doorbell rang. Startled by the unexpected sound, she shakily swiped at the tears and took a step forward. She didn't feel the glass shards piercing her feet until she took the second step. At that point, sharp pains shot through her foot. She gasped, then looked down in confusion. Her legs looked as if she'd been running through mud, and she was standing in broken glass and ice cream, while a thin ribbon of blood seeped out from beneath her toes.

"Oh, no," Nicole mumbled, then stifled a second moan of pain.

The doorbell rang again. She shivered, then clutched her head in confusion.

"Just a minute!" she yelled, then tried to sidestep the rest of the debris as she hobbled to the door.

When she looked through the peephole in the door, she didn't know whether to be relieved or regretful.

It was Dominic, and as usual, she was a mess.

Nicole smiled a little self-consciously as she opened the door to let him in. "I just don't know what's happening to me. I think I'm losing my mind."

"Hey, don't talk about my woman like that."

Nicole rode the surge of delight his words brought. "So I'm still your woman?"

Dominic lowered his head.

Their lips met.

The kiss proceeded.
Slowly.
Thoroughly.

* * * * *

Be sure to look for the
AFTERSHOCK *anthology next month,*
as well as other exciting paranormal stories
from Silhouette Nocturne.
Available in October wherever books are sold.

n o c t u r n e™

NEW YORK TIMES BESTSELLING AUTHOR

SHARON SALA

JANIS REAMES HUDSON
DEBRA COWAN

AFTERSHOCK

Three women are brought to the brink of death...
only to discover the aftershock of their trauma has
left them with unexpected and unwelcome gifts of
paranormal powers. Now each woman must learn to
accept her newfound abilities while fighting for life,
love and second chances....

Available October wherever books are sold.

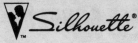

REQUEST YOUR FREE BOOKS!

2 FREE NOVELS PLUS 2 FREE GIFTS!

HARLEQUIN®

INTRIGUE®

Breathtaking Romantic Suspense

YES! Please send me 2 FREE Harlequin Intrigue® novels and my 2 FREE gifts (gifts are worth about $10). After receiving them, if I don't wish to receive any more books, I can return the shipping statement marked "cancel." If I don't cancel, I will receive 6 brand-new novels every month and be billed just $4.24 per book in the U.S. or $4.99 per book in Canada, plus 25¢ shipping and handling per book and applicable taxes, if any*. That's a savings of close to 15% off the cover price! I understand that accepting the 2 free books and gifts places me under no obligation to buy anything. I can always return a shipment and cancel at any time. Even if I never buy another book from Harlequin, the two free books and gifts are mine to keep forever.

182 HDN EEZ7   382 HDN EEZK

Name	(PLEASE PRINT)	
Address		Apt. #
City	State/Prov.	Zip/Postal Code

Signature (if under 18, a parent or guardian must sign)

Mail to the **Harlequin Reader Service:**
IN U.S.A.: P.O. Box 1867, Buffalo, NY 14240-1867
IN CANADA: P.O. Box 609, Fort Erie, Ontario L2A 5X3

Not valid to current subscribers of Harlequin Intrigue books.

Want to try two free books from another line?
Call 1-800-873-8635 or visit www.morefreebooks.com.

* Terms and prices subject to change without notice. N.Y. residents add applicable sales tax. Canadian residents will be charged applicable provincial taxes and GST. Offer not valid in Quebec. This offer is limited to one order per household. All orders subject to approval. Credit or debit balances in a customer's account(s) may be offset by any other outstanding balance owed by or to the customer. Please allow 4 to 6 weeks for delivery. Offer available while quantities last.

Your Privacy: Harlequin is committed to protecting your privacy. Our Privacy Policy is available online at www.eHarlequin.com or upon request from the Reader Service. From time to time we make our lists of customers available to reputable third parties who may have a product or service of interest to you. If you would prefer we not share your name and address, please check here. ☐

HI08R

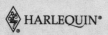
HARLEQUIN®

INTRIGUE®

COMING NEXT MONTH

#1089 CHRISTMAS SPIRIT by Rebecca York
A Holiday Mystery at Jenkins Cove
Some say old ghosts haunt Jenkins Cove, but not writer Michael Bryant. Can Chelsea Caldwell change his mind—or will ghosts of Christmas past drag the young couple to their doom?

#1090 PRIVATE S.W.A.T. TAKEOVER by Julie Miller
The Precinct: Brotherhood of the Badge
Veterinarian Liza Parrish was nobody special—until she witnessed the murder of KCPD's deputy commissioner. Now she had the city's finest at her disposal, but only needed their bravest, Holden Kincaid, to keep her from harm.

#1091 SECURITY BLANKET by Delores Fossen
Texas Paternity
Quinn "Lucky" Bacelli thought saving Marin Sheppard would be the end of their dalliance. But then she asked him for protection from her domineering parents. And to pretend to be the father of her infant son....

#1092 MOTIVE: SECRET BABY by Debra Webb
The Curse of Raven's Cliff
Someone had taken Camille Wells's baby. It was now up to recluse Nicholas Sterling III to help the woman he once loved and right his past wrongs if he was to save the town from the brink of disaster.

#1093 MANHUNT IN THE WILD WEST by Jessica Andersen
Bear Claw Creek Crime Lab
Federal agent Jonah Fairfax was in over his head, maintaining his cover in a Supermax prison. But when some escapees abducted Chelsea Swan, Jonah was ready to show his true colors in order to save the medical examiner's life.

#1094 BEAUTIFUL STRANGER by Kerry Connor
Doctor Josh Bennett couldn't deny a woman in distress. Now he had to help Claire Preston uncover the secrets of her past before a hired killer put them both down for good.

www.eHarlequin.com

HICNM0908